D0982219

"Armonía Somers is an extraordinary writer whose erotic fairy-tale world is akin to that of Angela Carter. Thanks to Kit Maude's perceptive rendering, the English-speaking reader can now discover one of the most original, and unfairly neglected, Latin American authors of the past century."

—ALBERTO MANGUEL,
author of *A History of Reading*

"Too strange and scandalous for her time, Somers is a feminist legend."

—LINA MERUANE,
author of *Seeing Red*

"This short but savage novel is essential reading. Hallucinatory, surreal, and beautifully brutal. Like a dream-vision that gets under your skin."

—JULIANNE PACHICO,
author of *The Lucky Ones*

THE NAKED WOMAN

THE NAKED

WOMAN

ARMONÍA SOMERS

Translated by Kit Maude
Afterword by Elena Chavez Goycochea

FEMINIST PRESS
AT THE CITY UNIVERSITY OF NEW YORK
NEW YORK CITY

Published in 2018 by the Feminist Press
at the City University of New York
The Graduate Center
365 Fifth Avenue, Suite 5406
New York, NY 10016

feministpress.org

First Feminist Press edition 2018

This book was made possible thanks to a grant from
New York State Council on the Arts with the support of Governor
Andrew M. Cuomo and the New York State Legislature.

This book is supported in part by an award from
the National Endowment for the Arts.

First printing November 2018

Cover and text design by Suki Boynton

Library of Congress Cataloging-in-Publication Data
Names: Somers, Armonía, author. | Maude, Kit, translator.
Title: The naked woman / Armonía Somers ; translated from the Spanish by
  Kit Maude.
Other titles: Mujer desnuda. English
Description: First Feminist Press edition. | New York, NY : Feminist Press at
  the City University of New York, 2018.
Identifiers: LCCN 2018018021 (print) | LCCN 2018021240 (ebook) | ISBN
  9781936932443 (ebook) | ISBN 9781936932436 (trade pbk.)
Classification: LCC PQ8519.S673 (ebook) | LCC PQ8519.S673 M8513
  2018 (print) | DDC 863/.64--dc23
LC record available at https://lccn.loc.gov/2018018021

THE NAKED WOMAN

As much as she'd been hoping otherwise, Rebeca Linke's thirtieth birthday began with exactly what she had expected: nothing. *What if nothing happens?* she asked herself. *I don't care if it's good or bad, so long as it's something.*

Her mistake had been to invest her hopes in a crucial event occurring at an arbitrary point in time when what needed to happen would inevitably be a flash in the dark, an unexpected ambush that catches you unawares during an otherwise ordinary situation.

But then the fateful day came. Just a dull summer yawn, as unremarkable as any other. Rebeca looked at it over her shoulder in the mirror. A beautiful day behind a beautiful face. Both lacking the qualities that make things memorable.

It all began with a subconscious withdrawal from her ordinary life, a disappearance. Perhaps the moment of revelation, when something truly unique happens in our lives, had finally come for her. If it occurs at a wake, this event consists of being full of life next to someone who will never move again. And if it marks the passing of yet another year, the kind involving a dangerously round number, it is the opportunity to finally decide what to do with the rest of your life.

The cottage at which Rebeca arrived at midnight seemed to be suspended in space. She hadn't got to know it yet. All she knew was what was in plain sight: a large field stretching out in front of her, abruptly interrupted by the dark silhouette of a sea creature. Right from the start, she thought that the forest looked like a beached whale. On the windy day she first saw it, it had been possessed by a kind of madness, like certain kinds of repressed human anger. The forest moved without moving, exhaling noisy, portentous gusts of wind, rooted to the spot in twitchy bondage. Then it would be still for a time, its indomitable mass breathing quietly.

To the right, the leafy barrier didn't quite reach the river. The river had no name, at least not one she knew, and ran along the forest, separated by a mysteriously clear strip of what was perhaps leaves or sand—something the color of her own personal void.

But there was more to the incredible landscape she had acquired upon buying the cottage for next to nothing. It was something less tangible, like the ability to escape at any moment by train. This is what had happened the night before when, watched in amazement by her fellow passengers, she had stepped off the train into the solitary locale: a stop in the middle of a field before the next station. She had been told it was a special privilege granted to the owner of the cottage. Well, if there was a reason for this odd addendum to her property rights, at that moment she wasn't interested in what it could be. She simply cut across the field lit by a complicit moon and slipped into the house, completely shorn of any ties to the past, feeling like she were entering a primitive womb from which she would only return once supremely well prepared.

Rebeca Linke let the coat covering her nudity fall to the floor. She lay on the bed and observed the moonlight filtering through the shutters; the black-and-white stripes made everything uniform. Several times she tried to close her eyes and slip between the bars, but they were waiting for her behind her eyelids. She became lost in a hypnotic dream. A dream that carried her back along the same rails as those used by the train that had stopped for her alone. Again she heard the insistent voice that had been badgering her since the beginning of her trip: "Excuse me, madam, can I see your ticket?" The man's heavy voice founders among the long, solid rows of seats. Trees line the road; another train passes in the opposite direction. After a long flight through the night, the stations come. People get on and off, stealing each other's places. "Haven't you found it yet?"

The man's voice upon her again. But she'll never find it. Then come the fences: taut, stretched wires, a monotonous hum. She tries to remember the title of the book on her nightstand and has to stammer, interrupted by the voice, which no longer comes from the man but the fences. "Allow me to look for it myself, madam. The ticket must be in your pocket, maybe next to your keys." This time the words sounded remote; the man had uttered them from among the far-off, trembling wires, as if through water, tangled in the violin strings vibrating in the static beyond life. "Oh, thank you," she said sweetly. "One always forgets the little things." Always forgets. Always forgets. Monotonous hum. The man's fingers wanted to take the music away from her. The key, the ticket, the fences. They pass over an iron bridge. The sound echoes in the chasm below. Someone cast into the void calls out sadly, "Madam, I don't want to interrupt your journey . . . but when someone sees trouble coming they should let others know . . . offer fair warning . . ." The last thing the little man will ever say. She would have liked to go back and jump out to find him. But the black-and-white stripes took her somewhere else, leaving her exhausted. "One always forgets the little things" was the last thing she could remember. "Always forgets." And yet, before passing out, she managed to remember other details. For example, inside the book on the nightstand there was a small dagger, a work of art, just right for beheading a woman imprisoned in irritating parallel bars like these. They were keeping her from finding herself.

The grasping hand won't make it. It knocks a glass of water off the table and sits there like a frozen flower. But then the dagger shows that it can reach her on its own. It moves, attracted to her fingertips and, of course, to her hand, which is attached to an arm, which in turn belongs to a body with a head and a neck. A head, such an important part of the body on top of something as fragile as a neck.

Although the arm was limp and the hand fingerless, the blade penetrated easily. It came across countless things that might have been called arteries, veins, cartilage, or warm, viscous blood, everything except for pain. By then, pain no longer existed.

The head rolled heavily, like a fruit. Rebeca Linke watched it fall impassively, feeling neither joy nor sorrow.

This marked the beginning of a new state of being, no more than a black strip, frozen definitively in time. Was it possible that the moving world had been resolved just like that, with a single thrust? The headless woman lay on the dark carpet, stretched out nightmarishly in her final act. There could be, there very well may be, a dimension in time for such things, but it offered little room for conjecture. Once the throat had been severed, all questions came to an end.

☾

Anyone who has ever lost a limb knows that on occasion, for a few brief titillating seconds, you feel as though it has returned. The sensation is very convincing. This is how she felt, still precariously placed in her memoryless strip. Or maybe her head, the one she didn't have, was sprouting again, easily, naturally, like a kind of poppy seed. She felt a slight buzzing inside of her, just a pregnant glimmer, but it was the only sign of life that she could have possibly hoped for.

After an incalculable period of time, deep, elemental impulses began to reappear. One foot twitched, then the whole body jerked upright, and just like that the black strip was tamed and the first stage was over. Now she was able to find her erstwhile head and take it in her hands. She rocked it gently as she walked, testing the weight of her burden. She was still unable to move in a set direction or keep her balance. An inner growth, like the first swelling of milk, was taking possession of her. But that wasn't all. In her deepest, most intimate core, an awareness of guilt started to manifest itself. She had spilled this sadness onto the earth; this head without a pedestal was her doing.

The woman could not yet do anything but the simplest acts, but she tried and succeeded in performing a series of movements. She picked up a handkerchief and placed it with her free hand under the head, fastening it at the bottom. This was more than necessary: blood was falling from the circular wound like rain.

Then the savage little statue shimmered back into reality and the true nature of her crime was revealed. But Rebeca Linke would never again try to balance out the two contradictory halves of herself. The only evidence of the poppy seed inside her was a muffled vegetable rattle, like hail hitting a windowpane. Although she was incapable of stringing together complex thoughts, she must have realized that this placid state could no longer be sustained. She was beholden to the present, like water held in the palm of a hand. Quickly placing the head on top of something, she stepped back to observe the effect in the darkness. The amputated body part continued to mutate, now adopting a stubborn disposition. Seen from a new perspective, the woman decided that she liked this version better than the little effigy of the peasant woman, with its round, protruding tongue. Fierce and angry from her chin to her eyebrows, temples, and hair, she regarded the incredible metamorphosis of the bodiless doll as a challenge. A strange, equivocal feeling came over her. She knelt down until she was at the same level as the head. "Amanda, I want to kiss you," she murmured. But she was unable to consummate the act. As in a nightmare, the unreality of her mouth made it impossible.

Suddenly, she saw in horror that the head was still bleeding, the gaunt, pale face hankering for its blood. It was now paramount that she restore the natural order of things. She had to bring her thoughts back to the top and reconstruct the real universe with its stars above and ground below. She had to rewrite the primordial plan. In one graceful movement, the decapitated woman picked up her old head and shoved it on like a helmet. The unfamiliar weight made her sway for a moment. It was difficult, annoying, to have to look at the world through eyes. She was trapped in an attic where things and their images scratched pitilessly at the innocent air, clamoring for their rightful places. Fortunately, the two flows of sap combined easily, far more quickly than would ordinarily happen in a grafted plant.

All fixed? The woman ran her thumbs around her neck, where the wound had started to burn like a red-hot wire, but this was nothing compared to the urgency of her new vigil. She stumbled around, surveying the room. In fact, the anemic head seemed changed, quite different. But what did that matter? A subtle feeling of happiness was distorting her ability to make the comparison. Finally, her hand, which was being unusually slow,

managed to get the door open. It had struggled
with the handle for an age.

☾

Out in the field, the woman's night, the first night
she had ever truly owned, began. Feeling dizzy,
she tried to grab hold of something to steady
herself, but there was nothing at hand. The stars
shone down on her, clustered tightly as though
their points had been soldered together. Even
after her embarrassing fall, she was still dazzled.
The night offered an unlimited opportunity to
fulfill her desires. She was much freer than those
sorry things in the sky—she was the night itself.
The woman had to get up and ignore the bram-
bles pricking the soles of her feet; the ground
looked softer further on. She'd never walked
barefoot before, not even on carpet or sand. But
she decided to accept the thorns without protest,
or at least as the stupid creatures they were: condemned to lie beneath her feet, always staring up
at the universe. Her hands were empty, and as
she continued walking, she decided to raise her
palms so she could read the lines in the moonlight. The fabulous fates that had once been read
there hesitantly, with an unnecessary amount of
melodrama, as though the fortune-teller were
unsure whether to reveal the complete truth,
were now impossible to decipher. It was strange:

she saw the old woman, the green eyes of a cat on her bony shoulder, the hanging jars, and the flowering branch across the window of the hut, but had not the slightest memory of the prophecy itself. All she knew was that it had been terrifying. She looked at the lines again the way a child who can't read has to make do with the pictures in a book, and yet she thought she saw something that she had never suspected her hands could harbor. She lowered them and caressed her hips. As she walked, she felt the hidden bones moving inside of her, so straight and covered so simply. She was taking stock of every detail to replace her old fear with an absolute disregard for danger. When she reached her breasts, she felt as if she were rediscovering herself after a long bout of amnesia. They had lost their former pertness, but their suggestive heft made them much more satisfying than before. She lifted one in each hand and walked on. Now the smooth field began, but it wasn't as soft or empty as it had seemed from afar. She was watched by hundreds of hidden eyes and chewed on by thousands of teeth. But this striking contrast, a true, genuine sensation, was alive beneath her feet. It flooded her body, filling it with messages.

Then came a new adventure: the forest. For a moment, the woman was stunned. The trees had sprung up suddenly, thick, dark, and rustling; she felt the sum of their breath on her face. She avoided them as best she could. Having walked thus far in a diagonal line, she found herself on the path of sand and leaves that separated the forest from the river. It was a relief to feel its soft bed, and she was tempted to lie down for a moment so she could look up at the sky without having to crane her neck. But suddenly, it seemed to her that the forest had recognized her, that it was spying on her. Either because she had grown used to the whispering or because it had stopped, she was swallowed by a brutal silence. She was lost in a mute, conspiratorial crowd.

"I'm as real as they are," she murmured to calm herself down. "Only more mobile. I can escape them and their buried feet . . ."

Nothing happened; not one of them had the initiative to uproot itself. She quickened her pace along the sand and soon her new haste developed into a wild run through the trees. Standing on their single stumps, they looked like a procession of casualties of war. The woman stopped again. If this expectant silence was for her, she thought, they could hear all they wanted to know then and there, not that she was feeling very inspired. "A brief life story," she said. "Enough to fill a small gravestone: Rebeca Linke, thirty years old. Left her personal life behind on a strange, timeless frontier." Nothing. That same old desolation, a clash of different languages and customs. "Maybe things are looking for their origins," she continued, still embittered by the curse of culture. She turned her floating head away and started walking again. With her new approach to life, nothing could upset her anymore, not even the mythical serpent, now old and no doubt toothless, even if he was still trying to play his game. As the owner of the night, she had no interest in ancient history, especially now that she knew it ended with the sorry chapter of modernity. Now that she had broken with the past, she was met with a vision of normalcy, the simple sleep of the common man, his confident snoring beating out a rhythm from the pillow. Others just like him would be doing the same, filling the earth's night with noise from their prone heads next to their conscious, insomniac wives. *How could anyone*, she thought, *especially the ruler of paradise — a being so full of wisdom and destiny — dare to use the excuse of such remote sin to arrange things so that these women lie awake next to sleeping men?*

In the meantime, she had covered a sizable distance. This was probably the only benefit of thinking back to an absurd story that hardly applied to her. But, of course, she mustn't try to tie up the loose ends: therein lay the danger. "Danger." She said the word disdainfully, like a bird swaying on a creaking branch.

She was about to set foot on a cultivated patch of land when she saw a log cabin rise up from the earth. The moon loomed above the squat, fragile dwelling as in an illustration for a fairy tale.

The half-open door gave the cabin an inviting air in spite of its crude construction. The woman slipped in sideways so as not to give herself away with the creak of hinges and entered a space that appeared to have carved out its own slice of calm. For a few moments, she was unable to move. She could barely see the brighter shapes of the back windows, but she could hear the throbbing of a pair of lives, each with its own respiratory system. One was deep and intense, panting in tune with the forest; the other weak and stuttering, now and again coming to a complete stop in a kind of death rattle. Then there was an agonizing squeak, and the faltering breath began again, scrabbling at the air, clinging on by its fingernails. She followed this counterpoint of breathing right to the center of the room. Once her eyes had adjusted to the light, she was able to make out the sleepers. They were gone from this world, sleeping the sacred sleep of beasts of burden whose only respite is the collapse at the end of the day.

These sleeping creatures were the very embodiment of indifference, maybe the same indifference as that she had left behind in the forest, on the train, and in the streets, plazas, and stores of the city before that. An indifference she could invariably detect wherever she was. This time, however, she decided to take the initiative and lie down on the side where life seemed strongest, just to see what would happen.

The man hardly stirred. He turned a little to accommodate this new, unexpected triangle, one side of which came from another world. His lungs continued their work and she had to adapt to their rhythm. Every time he breathed in, sucking up almost all the air in the cabin, she accompanied the cyclone, struggling in the current like an insect caught in the plumbing. Then she was unceremoniously vomited out, only to be drawn back in again. This was a wonderful game, joined with the inertia of a light object floating on the tide. She could have played it all night long or for the rest of her life. But then it was ruined. She had started to touch the man's naked chest, which was embedded with a strange mat of hair, rough and short, like horsehair.

"What is it, who's there?" he mumbled in his sleep, his tongue prickling like it was swarming with ants.

"It's me, Eve," the woman whispered in the same strange, unfamiliar voice with which she had spoken to the trees.

The man tried to open his eyes, but his eyelids felt as heavy as lead weights.

"Antonia . . . leave me alone . . ." he said, his words hindered by something deep inside of him.

"How awful, whose name is that?"

"Yours, damn it. Come on . . . stop it . . . I've told you before . . ."

"No, that dreadful name doesn't belong to me. Women shouldn't have names that can be made masculine by changing a couple of letters. The truly feminine ones are unique unto themselves. Like all my names," said the stranger, whispering warmly into his ear.

"And what are they?" he asked, growing accustomed to a dialogue that may or may not have been taking place in his mind.

"Eve, Judith, Semiramis, Magdala. And to a man who dreamed of a foot that was centuries older than he, my name is Gradiva, the woman who walks."

"Eve, Gradiva," he repeated; it was all he could do to remember the first and last of the series. "What the hell do you want? Tell me or I'll throw you out of bed," he added coarsely.

"I don't know exactly," she answered. "Come, touch me, I'm naked. I claimed my freedom and went outside. I have done without codes and the thorns cut me for it. The forest blew its breath in my face; the serpent tried to repeat that sordid old story with the fruit. It was all the same as before, when I belonged to them. But now you're alone with me, even if she is over there breathing so strangely. She belongs to you but you don't care about her; she is like so many of my own. I want to know how I would be, how all the women inside of me would be with you. What I am saying to you is so simple and yet so complicated, I know that, my poor darling. But you don't need to understand. It will all be better that way, its full meaning beyond you."

The woman's voice came out hot and soft as newly shed ash. He could feel her physically at his ear but he also heard her inside of him, and this dual sensation gave rise to yet another: the wonderfully strange feeling of having someone inside your body.

"Woman . . . what . . . you're always so quiet, and now you're talking like this . . . This isn't like you, Antonia . . ."

"No, no, no! If you touch me, you'll see that I'm someone else. If you smell my hair, or underneath my arms, you'll find that we're two very different women," she protested.

The man, like someone recovering from the effects of anesthesia, was now becoming dangerously agitated. He was going to end up ruining everything, both his woodsman's peace and the dream of love that had descended upon his pillow. She started to feel anxious about their ill-advised encounter. It was going to be the same old story: possessions shared out of fear, deceit and thievery, repellant clothes covering her once more. She barely hesitated. Quickly, she placed her feet back on the ground and crossed the room, knocking something over as she went, and slipped back out into the night that had unleashed her madness.

The woodsman sighed, suddenly awake. He was sweating from head to toe, his mouth was dry, and his blood was pounding rebelliously, like a slave uprising in a tunnel. He turned over and touched a skinny body with clumsy fingers. As always, his wife was there and yet only present in the most basic sense of the word: cold and entirely unresponsive. But now the man's desire had swelled like a river after the rainy season.

"Antonia," he begged in a thick voice, "give me your body face up. It's come back, give it to me, give it to me."

Even though she was awake, she didn't obey.

He brutally turned her over, forcing his wife into position like an animal. She didn't have the strength or will to resist.

"Eve, Eve, damn you and your dreams. What were the other names you said? Yes, look: now I want to. Now I can. Open those legs or I'll chop them off. Let me do this. Now, I can't stand it," he whined, his body writhing in anguish, taking control of the withered human form before him.

"Have you lost your mind? My God!" Antonia choked, her throat tied up in knots.

"Yes, yes, I have," he panted without stopping. "That's what you said to me one night, remember? Thirty years ago, when you put the bouquet of flowers on the table and I tore off your tight, white dress. That time you tricked me, pretending to be so stupid. You didn't want it then either, you said, but you had a fire inside of you. It didn't last long, of course. But it was real fire, you old bitch, you hid the flames under the surface, you fucking whore. Get moving, just once, like that time . . . I'd kill to get you to do it one more time before we die . . . but now I have to beg you for it like a fool. I'd lick your bones where I've dug in my nails just to get you to act a little like that day . . ."

A pristine memory, thought the poor trembling woman superstitiously, that should never be profaned, not even by them. She struggled weakly to defend it: she still had the moth-eaten flowers and torn dress. But he held her more firmly, taking even that lost moment protected from the folds of time away from her. He hacked away at her as if she were a tree trunk. The deathly, living trance was terrible for the woman to bear. She was as impervious to the flames as sodden wood. It was all she could do to smoke a little in protest.

"No, Nathaniel, stop! You're hurting me! Stop it, you bastard!" She was amazed to hear herself scream, as though her voice had been taken over by somebody else.

But the man went on, deaf to the world, trapped in his own net, governed entirely by the imperative to keep thrusting. He was oblivious to everything else, even the inert, pale, suffering body he was assaulting. There was no room for pity, only this blind act of annihilation and the final embers of a torch that had slowly been going out without his realizing. All this was happening independently of him, as though it were beyond his control, with the fatality of a landslide. He let himself ooze out, drop by drop, in brief shudders of desperation and triumph expressed in the anachronistic language of another time relived through his present sacrifice. Then, after delivering himself entirely, he fell back, unconscious, damp, and lost. Only after a few minutes was he able to say anything intelligible.

"Antonia, was that really you talking to me in the middle of the night?"

His voice sounded distant, as if from a more humble creature, far more restrained than the man of a few minutes ago.

"I'm going to make a cup of chamomile tea" was all she said in reply, smothering her hatred in an ancient, bestial servitude.

She dragged herself along on bare feet, turned on the light, and started to rummage through the pots and pans. The man, meanwhile, lay back in his usual position, staring up at the ceiling. Suddenly, sick of the beams he'd been counting for thirty years without ever finding one out of place, he rolled onto his stomach. And then, like a stone thrown through a window, he let out a primitive, feral roar, shaking the cabin to its very foundations. By the simple means of his nasal passages, he had discovered how a being chained to reality for many years could break free of its shackles. The amazing thing was that it had left its mark without him or anyone else noticing. It had lain next to his body unseen, like a funeral rose sinking its roots into the body of the deceased. And he had raised himself from the dead to smell the flowers that were still very much alive above him.

"No, woman, I don't want any more of your concoctions!" he shouted, sitting up in bed. "She, I don't know who she was, but she was real, she was right here next to me. Come over here, if you don't believe me. Don't just stand there like a scarecrow, come and sniff these sheets. Is it your dirty, smoky hair? Are you so afraid of bending over? Smell, you wretched thing, smell and then crumble away once and for all. Leave me alone with these sheets!"

He plunged his nose back into the indentation, trying to inhale as much of the absent woman as he could. At times, he lost the trail of her essence in the fury of his lungs. Then he began to breathe in more gently, as he never had in his boorish life. But his wife made no effort to find out what he was talking about. She stood there stupidly, staring at him with the mug in her hand. Then, overwhelmed by the crazed scene taking place in their cabin, her fingers went limp and it fell to the ground. It was the sight of something so real being smashed to pieces that convinced the man once and for all. Something had broken. He'd heard it. Clay fragments lay on the ground, the evidence stuck in his brain like shrapnel. Meanwhile, the smell of the woman from his dream taunted him; it was so close and yet he couldn't satisfy his desires in his pillow or escape from the temptation lurking in the folds of the sheets. He leaped away from the source of his torment, opened the door to a night slowly fading into dawn, and began to scream into the forest, "Eve! Eve! Eve!"

❨

Back on the soft path that separated the trees from the river, the woman left the cabin behind without ever turning back, not even to check if it had been real. She wasn't about to wallow in her failure. She had been a guest there and had wanted, demanded even, something they didn't know how to give her. But the accounts she would later offer of her adventure would focus not on the man's frustration but the ruthlessness with which she had exposed his impotence. This was how she would debunk certain myths. The man hadn't laid a finger on her and yet she had been far from chaste. It was a question of full- or half-blooded desire: that was the key. But even this discovery had no effect on her new perspective. Ever since she had lost her conventional consciousness, she had moved freely, without hindrance. *What a useless invention consciousness is*, she thought. She would have preferred a different approach to such an awful concept, something more firmly based in tangible fact. But that would require abstract theory, the reduction of one's personal experience to generalized norms that, whether they were shared or rejected, would nonetheless eventually come to apply. And thence the falsities, the need to be trusted, and all those wretched domestic games would begin all over again.

Her attention was drawn to the noise of the river, now close by. She was in no hurry to get anywhere, so she flopped down onto the sand. Her breasts felt heavy and painful, scratched by the branches that had blocked her way. But, physically, she was still fine. Her persistence was like that of certain memories that linger uselessly in the widowed soul. In her languid position, she thought back over the episode with the woodsman, the mature beauty to which he was oblivious and the jail cell in which he lived, unaware he was a prisoner. Then there was the clumsy confusion of bodies into which she had stumbled, how he had pawed the worn reality of a remembered name while she whispered a procession of infamous women in his ear. She laughed out loud at the contrast. But fortunately the chapters in which she reconstructed the story were already more confused than even a minute ago. Their outlines blurred, faded, and were superimposed over each other as they drifted further and further away from their point of origin. Then her attention was diverted to a new character slithering a few steps away, and she was able to rid herself of the last remnants.

The river's sudden appearance promised far more than its current alone. It was a long, living creature lying on its back with something solitary and incomprehensible dissolved in its marrow. She stood up and walked across the pebbly shore, fully aware of the commotion she was causing: she was an alien element in a strange land. Intrepid creatures leaped out from the undergrowth in front of her. One soared in a perfect parabola before falling into the water, filling the surface with circular ripples. But she knew that the apparent inoffensiveness of the scene wasn't the whole story. Something out there was coming to an end. As she continued, guided by a nameless compass, the river flowed on, progressively less oblivious, chaste, and innocent than it had been at its source. It betrayed a kind of animal anxiety, a painful bewilderment mixed with denial. She wanted to find out why but was unable to establish a dialogue with the creature, nor it with her. Perhaps it wanted her to go away, to be left alone with a secret invisible to her or anyone with mobile eyes. It was then she realized that dawn was breaking over the water, and felt a shiver of fear. Her nudity and commitment to freedom had begun at night, when morning had been unimaginable. But a sunny morning was settling over the land, and she was entirely unprepared to deal with the light. Not even memories from her former existence helped. She had no name, origin, or explanation—an oppressive triumvirate that always led back to the same place.

Behind her, she thought as she walked, the established order must go on repeating itself until it's worn out, with never a new idea to replace it. A fuzzy memory of the man from the cabin came to her. She had seen him for the last time as a ghostly form in the fog. Maybe now he was awake. She had knocked something over as she left and hadn't closed the door. This evidence meant he wouldn't be able to dismiss her as a dream. But there was nothing left to say except *What do I care?* Like a boy trying to get over being punished by his father, she shrugged her shoulders at the episode in the woods: the universal sign of indifference. She walked on, the milky air descending around her.

❬

The woodsman was a short, stocky, thick-necked fellow; the straw-colored hair on his head, face, and chest was turning white. The fury of the search had shot blood into his blue eyes, and his body was covered in sweat, earth, and small leaves.

"Stop, Nathaniel. Forget this ridiculous dream, I beg you," said his wife, who was following him like a shadow.

But he went on running through the forest,

ricocheting off trees and shoving branches out of his way. From his dry throat came the wild, demonic whine of a dog on the trail of its prey. As he entered a clearing, he stumbled over the trunk of a tree he had chopped down the day before, but he pulled himself back upright out of sheer tenacity and continued his mad search.

"She must have sheltered here in the night," he said to himself. "She couldn't have swum the river or crossed the field, at least not if she was naked as I remember. She said she was. What was she doing? Where was she going?"

He regarded his wife's approach with a mixture of anger and contempt. She was covered in a shoddy, dirt-colored dress. Her gray hair, tied loosely with a bow, might have given her an unreal air from far away, blending in with the bark of the trees. But no, she was on a blind mission as well, apparently bent on her own destruction. She seemed determined to force him to look at her ruined body. There was no way to stop her. Suddenly, she was standing right in front of her husband, superimposed over the image of the other woman, which still lingered in the man's mind like a comet's tail. "It's like the mark left by a painting on the wall, when no one can remember what on earth the picture was," he grumbled before spitting. "But thankfully she won't talk. She's not used to it, I broke her many years ago," he said, sitting down on the fallen tree.

He stared at her, gasping for breath, and realized for a brief, amazed second that he was only now seeing her for what she was: an alien from a distant planet. He had never noticed how merciless the ravages of time had been upon her.

"Yes, Nathaniel, you know it's true," she said in a grandmotherly voice. Sitting down next to him, she placed a weightless hand on his knee. "It wasn't a dream. You woke up early this morning doing unspeakable things, things that make me ashamed just to remember them. My God. But now the sun has come out, and you and I are here, wide awake, sitting on this tree you felled yesterday with the tools you use every day . . ."

It was the wrong thing to say. The stranger she was trying to mollify with soothing words and gestures stood up and walked over to his ax. He picked it up with both hands and faced the terrified, ancient child who was trying to restore his sanity. Yes, he shouted, his throat hoarse with the effort, she needed to learn once and for all that she would never be able to change his mind. She'd better remember that if she didn't want him to chop her down on the spot and leave her rotting under the dry leaves on the forest floor. He resumed his search for the lost trail, muttering to himself. Every word he uttered in a futile effort to bring back the other woman plunged the person next to him deeper and deeper into a pit of despair: "Eve, Eve . . . I know now that your scent was different, under your arms and in your hair. Your accursed smell mixed with the crushed flowers sticking to your skin. You asked me to smell you, to remember it all with my dead, piggish nostrils. Then there was everything else: Your fingers on my chest. The names I can't remember, the names that can never be male that you whispered in my ear in your secret voice. My darling bitch of youth, my sweet whore from another time . . ."

☾

The woman stopped abruptly. She was being watched. Not in the usual way, she noticed immediately, when a connection forms between the person looking and the subject of their gaze, but as though through a one-way mirror. Finally, she spotted the little woman. She'd been placed in an absurd niche cut into a pole, a house without a door always facing in the same direction, as though the sun, moon, and flowers behind her didn't exist. The Virgin appeared to acquiesce to her plight with a fixed smile, and the woman realized in terror that the face looking down at her was hers from another era. It was her own unmoving body that was stuck in place, forever facing a single direction. The woman turned away and headed out into the field.

And then the real danger began. The flat terrain and strengthening light made her a perfect target with no possibility of escape. Two men appeared in the distance sitting on top of a single horse. The encounter hardly came as a surprise to the woman—it was logical for them to be there—but it was very different for the men. Although they could barely make out the shape in the early morning light, they knew very well that there had never been a tree in the spot where one now appeared to be standing. They stopped to get a better look and saw that the tree seemed to have pulled up its roots and was now on the move. They rode forward. The tree began to grow lighter, as though caught in its own personal midsummer snowstorm. As the ghostly object and the men drew together, the number of words they were capable of uttering from their open, drooling mouths dwindled.

The two men were more or less identical twins. Both were medium-sized blonds with an embryonic gaze that gave them a stupid, uncooked air. Craning their necks to see better, riding closer and closer in the morning light, they made their grand discovery: a naked woman in the middle of the field! They sat stock-still, their necks stretched out as far as they could go. It wasn't a ghost or a tree, but a real woman, with long, loose hair and arms down at her sides.

Of course, this was something that all men, when dying of boredom, mad with lust, tormented by adolescence or the like, have imagined happening to them at some point in their lives.

A wonderful woman such as this springing up from the earth, or appearing in the bathroom, or in the window across the road, offering herself in apparent supplication, ready to satisfy their every bodily desire. But these circumstances were rather different; she dazzled the mind with her shocking reality, from her torso to her fingernails. Then, as they got even closer, they saw her impenetrable eyes, whose twinkling light spiraled down inside of her. She was tired, her body crisscrossed with cuts, but she looked so diaphanous against the dark earth, thought the yokels—or they would have if they had been capable of such eloquence—and so confident; defiant but tranquil.

She regarded them indulgently, instinctively understanding them in their stupidity. Although she wasn't much older than they were, she could draw on the accumulated experience of countless previous incarnations.

"May I cross this field?" she asked humbly, more to jolt them out of their stupor than to really ask permission.

The tangibility of her voice, the first real proof that she was actually there, was too much. Their only answer was to jump nimbly off their horse, one to either side, and run off back along the furrow they had been plowing. They moved so fast that they left no footprints, as though they were running away from the devil himself.

The woman stood next to the horse, utterly

alone. Situated between her and the fleeing twins, the animal soon came to stand for all of existence. She had never seen or felt a horse at such close quarters. Its straw-colored hair, musky, slightly rotten smell, and the dampness of its eyes and snout made it the absolute embodiment of life. She could see evidence of it throbbing throughout its body. In certain areas under the beast's sweaty skin, the pulsing grew more impatient, but the horse stood there, unmoving, waiting for who knows what, entirely disconnected from this inner flow, as though they were two separate entities. She clumsily set it free, fumbling as if she were undressing a newborn baby for the first time. "Why do people find it so difficult to do these things? Why are they so hard to do?" she asked the horse repeatedly during the process. Then she saw the blood: a wound inflicted by the halter stood out brightly against its skin. A fly noticed it at the same time and buzzed over to sit next to the gash. Disgusted though she was by its interminable sucking, she didn't look away. She knew the men were going to come back. They had gone in search of something with which to shore up their fear and locate their courage, something that might miraculously puff out their sunken chests. But not even the knowledge that she was running out of time could drag her eyes away from the wound, even when her fascination was accompanied by a fly and its desperate coupling. Of course, it would be far too generous to just hand herself over to them. The twins would describe her nakedness vividly and a crowd would come after her. But they weren't yet aware of the ancient source of her confidence. Aggravated by the sun and the fly's thirst, the cut seemed to have grown into a trench around her feet, blocking her way. Driven by an uncontrollable urge, she kissed it. She barely had any saliva left under her tongue, but she gathered enough to make a ritual offering—in any other situation it would have seemed entirely out of place. It was in the midst of this act that she remembered with a start the danger she was in.

"They're coming, aren't they?" she asked the animal, stroking the painful area around the irritated flesh. "Yes, there's no doubt about it; many more pairs of eyes will come and they'll judge me in their murky ignorance and brash stupidity."

The animal looked at her quizzically from under its gray-blond eyelashes, an old curtain that had long forgotten how to shed its dust.

"But no, that won't happen, don't worry," she reassured herself. "I'll escape. No matter how slim my chances, I'll get away. Right from under their noses."

She would have liked to venture something more calculated, maybe a whole defensive strategy, but she was heading into unknown territory. For reasons she didn't quite understand, she was unable to marshal the kind of ideas—like ants marching grimly along in single file—that lead to concrete actions. Coherent thoughts eluded her. She must be guided by yes-or-no decisions, she told herself, without examining this line of reasoning too closely. She looked at the horse again, relishing the uncertainty. The only proof that life went on as usual was the sound of its teeth munching the grass. She had in no way affected its primitive plans.

"If anything, anything at all, occurs as it should, like a planet following its orbit, it is because God approves," she declared, setting off quickly to make up for lost time.

Her scandalous amorality, like acid in a jeweler's dark workshop, dissolved all that was worthless before it had a chance to sully the precious metal. "Either this is the summer sun or the gold that appears at the end of the process," she told herself, sprinting across the warm field like a white mare.

☾

By now, the alarm had been raised throughout the village nearby. The high-pitched, hysterical squeals of the twin brothers were drowned out by the voices of the local residents, whose doors all opened at once as though blown out by a supernatural earthquake. The houses were not large; despite their conventional little gardens, the customary single tree in front, and their naive checkerboard layout, they weren't entirely lacking in charm. The entire village seemed to have come into being all at once to meet a collective need that had no time for the niceties of urban planning. Beyond were the fields of labor, which had a somewhat picture-postcard look. Behind were the cowsheds, a major part of the lives of each family group. The distinctive smell of the village emanated from them: a compelling cloud of maternity, milk, straw, and manure. Nearby, separated by a rarely used path (the main street to the train station led everywhere) were neglected vegetable gardens. They had belonged to a previous generation of settlers, whose fate was a mystery. The new arrivals had allowed them to run wild, unable to decide whether to turn them over for grazing or tend them. Maybe they were keeping them in reserve for future municipal growth. It was in this very ordinary place, where the only things that ever happened were the milking of cows, the delivery of pails of milk to the milk train, the sowing of crops, the act of marriage, and the bearing of children who would grow up to do exactly the same ordinary things—which also included going to church on Sunday, dying, and passing on one's surname—that the first thing of consequence they had ever experienced beyond their poverty of spirit occurred. The news borne by the twins began to spread.

One man, the first to hear said news, took the precaution of grabbing his pitchfork. This act was significant in that it served as an example. More men emerged from doors and milking stalls, initially empty-handed given the nature of the news, but when they saw that their neighbors were armed, they ran back inside and returned with hoes, shovels, rakes, and whatever else they could lay their hands on. Then they strode forward with their weapons on their shoulders, barking instructions and shooing the women and children inside. Some primal instinct told them that they had been drafted into a private war, in which the opposite sex and the young would only be a hindrance.

Soon the barbarian army was fully assembled. It seemed very important that they head out on their expedition en masse. Although the bounty would ultimately be individual, or at least impossible to divvy up, a sense of victory could still be shared and the presence of so many men served as justification in itself: they were a united front. No one quite knew who it was that might be judging them, but their numbers undoubtedly helped keep the fear nipping their ankles at bay.

Eventually, the procession arrived at the epicenter of the phenomenon: the place where the twins had left their plough and horse, and where they expected to find the stranger and her shameful femininity, her arms across her chest and her eyes pleading. But what they found instead left them astounded; the look the rubbernecked twins exchanged was a fair indication of the general sense of awe. There were no opportunities here for prurience or sainthood, only the rather different, robust image of a horse that had been set free and was busy grazing, whisking flies away with its tail. Although their private fantasies had been dashed, it was only now that the story became truly real for them, for now it had actual substance. Something conjured up in the minds of the twins couldn't possibly have removed the harness from the horse. That would have meant missing out on a day of the only work they were capable of doing, not to mention laying themselves open to general ridicule.

One man, who was well versed in crime literature (a mysterious package of books would often arrive for him at the train station), made his way through the crowd, saying words that nobody could understand but the smartest among them believed to be related to something beyond the comprehension of the ordinary man. They opened a path for him in the same way that people do when someone declares, "I'm a doctor," thus immediately earning themselves a greater say over the patient gasping on the ground. The man, enjoying his sudden prominence, started to examine the rudimentary wooden plough, a contraption that must have represented the earliest stage of the tool's evolution. Ignoring the crudeness of the implement, he ran his hand over every part, inspecting each joint and rivet as though he were coaxing out their secrets. He did so with a specialist's touch, very different from the rough, utilitarian motions of ordinary labor. This demonstration of analytical expertise, not dissimilar to the way a blind person becomes familiar with an object, was a revelation to many. They realized that even an insignificant tool, a two-cent plough, was built according to a plan, by an intelligence that was also capable of creating a gun, a table, or a milking machine. Each part was built for a purpose that would be repeated over and over again. The investigator, oblivious to the admiration he was arousing among some for the very first time, suddenly bent over to focus all his attention on a fixed point. On the horizontal axis of the bar to which the harness was tied, caught at the corner where it met a vertical plank, something was glinting insolently in the sun. The tip of a woman's nail, painted with red nail polish. The man extracted the tiny shard with the delicacy of a watchmaker removing a hair from the mechanism. Then he held it out in his palm for all to see. He finished his demonstration by wrapping it carefully in a handkerchief.

"Proof of feminine clumsiness when handling a harness," he remarked from a higher plane than that of mere mortals. The others were left open-mouthed at the effectiveness of his methodology.

In fact, this was the first time any of them had

seen such an act firsthand. Given the dearth of extraordinary experiences in their everyday lives, the feat assumed the status of a magic trick or some other wonderful surprise. But their amazement didn't last long.

"At the end of the day, we're just wasting time sniffing around worthless objects," said a member of the group. The voice was that of the deacon, who'd brought the torch used to light the candles for mass.

Worn out and frustrated by the investigator's meticulous examination, the men quickly shuffled away before it could go on any longer, and began to split up in different directions. Some went off on their own while others formed groups based around shared theories they had discussed on the way there. They went toward the river, into the forest, and to the haystacks that had burned down a few days before, next to the railroad. The sun, meanwhile, continued to rise, sinking its yellow teeth deep into the earth, as one of the men put it before letting loose a stream of blasphemy that earned the opprobrium of the others. They felt that there was enough sin in the air as it was.

"Forget the sun, you'll get used to it," said a little man who had been trembling the entire time. "I'm thinking of my wife, damn it. What will she do if this woman turns up at our house to ask for clothes or to use the bathroom?"

"Just yours?" asked the man closest to him with

a laugh that attracted several more curious onlookers. "Listen to him, just *his* wife, he says. They'll all be at it, even the ones who were kind enough to make us widowers. They'll be scratching at the earth, desperate to stab her eyes out with the very scissors that killed them or to throw boiling milk on her," he went on, forgetting his grief, which had moved the entire village for quite some time.

For a few seconds, the widower had the feeling that he'd disgraced himself, leaving him susceptible to a judgment that would rain down upon his head as copiously as the consolation that had once come his way even after his tears had come to an end. But nothing happened. The dirty business in which they were all involved seemed such a grand undertaking that they could now accept that one's widowerhood eventually comes to an end, reduced simply to a marital status only of interest to the census taker. But this was nothing compared to other, even more incredible developments. For instance, men looking under tiny shrubs, like they were searching for a partridge or rabbit, escaped the customary jeers and stones. Instead of mockery, they would be joined by someone else, thus made to feel less ashamed of their stupidity.

They spent the entire morning in this manner, but their long hours of toil resulted only in disappointment. At midday, they returned to their homes in defeat, sweating copiously, and ate their lunch without saying a word about the affair. They could be sure of one thing: she was as real as the sliver of a nail, but nowhere to be found.

The search continued in the afternoon. By then the Naked Woman was on everyone's lips. The policeman, the priest, the doctor, and the schoolchildren were either asking for more information or inventing their own. Obviously, nobody thought of looking for her closer to home, in the old vegetable gardens. *She must have fled*, they thought. They needed to expand the search on all sides.

But they didn't dare put the plough horse back in its harness; they left it where it was while the man who had found the nail handed it in at the tiny police station.

❦

"Don't close that door, close the one to the children's room," the man said grumpily, taking off a shirt that had been reduced to a hot rag and throwing it across the room.

"But, Juan, it's the front door. You always make sure that I remember to lock it before I go to bed," his wife protested with an artificial cheeriness she had adopted for the occasion.

"Not that one, I said, just leave it open," the man growled, grinding his teeth over the last few words. "Lock the one to the children's room. Double, triple lock it, lock it as many times as you want, and let that be an end to it. We're not going to spend all night playing this stupid game. I'm not going to argue about doors until dawn."

He was issuing these orders about which door to lock and which to leave open—an unprecedented concern in village life—sitting half-naked on the bed. Their bickering had soured the air throughout the house, overpowering the smell of recently finished dinner.

His wife, thrown by this sultry new atmosphere, spent several minutes regarding her husband in a new light. He had a gleaming, reddish mat of hair on his chest; the hair on his head was similar but fading. His wiry, young body and velvety hair, she thought, didn't match his words. Something strange was happening to him, but he seemed completely unaware of it. This commanding, late-night voice transformed his physique into something wild and a little monstrous, lending his body an intangible strength that coursed through his veins. It was impossible to describe in words, but if someone were forced to, they'd need the vocabulary of a great novelist, the kind who wrote the books she had read in her youth, when she had been dazzled by the many-colored, mosaic-like arrangements that could be made from the raw material other people used only for speech. But still she arrived at a truth: an explanation for what was going on. It wasn't like the cheap romances she'd read, but the stuff legends are built on. Of course, the same thing must be happening in every other house in the village, she thought solemnly. All the men were leaving their front doors ajar, just in case the devilish woman came by looking for refuge, honest bread, and white milk. Juan's wife knew this very well, as did all the other women, and she almost said so. She was tempted to climb up onto the nearest gate and proclaim that her feminine counterpart had become an obsession throughout the day. The men, even the most rustic and tranquil among them, had started to feel that old anxiety once more, like frogs caught on barbed wire. The twins' description had been unimaginative enough for their dull brains to tailor it to their own personal fantasies. "A completely naked woman with a soft voice and long hair," they'd said over and over again. "No, she was classy," they'd responded to more specific questions. "She had red nails and a slim neck." The blunt simplicity of this information left a blank slate on which each man could draw his own picture. "The images in their minds," she mumbled to herself, still standing, "may all have been different, but they were still plotting the same betrayal." She turned to her husband. He looked like a statue: elbows on his knees, head in his hands. *A kaleidoscopic world for two cents. That was all, the few coins one was able to scrabble together years ago. And yet, what a range of colors and flavors was available. The perfect exhilaration of being single . . . I have no idea what he's thinking, I can't get it out of him. A thought like that isn't like a chicken's giblets, you can't just dig it out after the poor bird's been cut open like a street dug up for waterworks.*

Oblivious to his wife's thoughts, the man was enjoying himself once again, reliving every second of a life that had gone up in smoke from one day to the next. It had transformed into the mortal labor of a worm wriggling in cheese, forever immersed in the same smell, the same taste, the same fate as the one next to it. But then one day the woman had come along to make everything new again, showing that the cheese could be cut open and the gorging serfs tossed out onto the ground. They'd die eating dirt if they had to, but first they'd breathe in, savor, and see everything that she, a woman without clothes walking in the sun, had brought from paradise. Then he took his hands from his eyes and sat blinking for a few moments. It was a long shot, he told himself. He'd regret it tomorrow. He was used to planning out every act he made in the life that had been allotted to him.

"Hey, what are you doing there, you fool? What on earth are you up to? And what am I doing sitting here like a cripple? Waiting for someone to come help undress me?" he shouted suddenly, standing up. "I was talking to you about doors, I think. Not flies or the dust in the air."

He furiously tore off his pants, or rather emerged from them. His calves were as firm as the rest of his body, but also delicate, a sharp contrast to his grotesque barking.

"But why, Juan?" she asked again, maintaining her cheery mask. "The children might start crying, you know they often do, and we wouldn't hear them. Don't forget the baby is susceptible to hernias . . ."

But before she could finish her next maternal argument, that the baby was too fragile to be left alone, she came to a realization. Enough of these tricks, they would have no effect on her man—he was lost already. Every woman knows when she's gone as far as she can. Like getting out of bed in the dark, the lights out, and running into a door or piece of furniture, the sensation occurs in many different ways and applies to many different things. This time it was his command that they close themselves off from the innocence sleeping next door. She sensed that instead of their usual measured contact, she was about to be ravaged in the name of his desire. But how much did that desire have to do with her?

"Clothes off and lights out! Do you hear me? Now!"

"Juan, my God! You're scaring me!"

"I want you naked, but I don't want to see you. Quickly, if you don't want me to tear your clothes off myself and wake the children while I'm at it."

Now it was all out in the open: she'd been replaced by another woman and humiliated besides, reminded that she was just a poor working woman, the mother of two children. But he didn't want her to let on that she knew. He wanted her to lie still on the bed like a stone. A bed smelling of the apples with which she always perfumed the wardrobe. He'd force her to do who knows what, blushing invisibly in the dark. But she also knew there was no point resisting. The Naked Woman had gotten into the blood of this rough creature, and he'd have his way no matter what. The same thing was happening behind closed doors throughout the village, a return to something with as many names as moods. They thought that the simplicity of their lives had killed it off forever, but nine months from now the village would be overwhelmed with crying babies. *The priest won't have enough holy water for all the baptisms*, she thought. *We'll have to expand into the old vegetable gardens*. Finally, the land they'd controversially set aside for the future, which so many of them hadn't seen the point of, would have a purpose. The red-hot night of the woman, she concluded, slowly undoing her robe, will eclipse the effort of thousands of restrained evenings during which the women, instinctive economists, went about rationing chastity and lust so as to ensure that the community grew in a measured, orderly way.

This scene occurred throughout the village with the jarring inevitability of a natural disaster. But as this strange night went on behind doors universally left unlocked, something else began to happen to the men that they were at a loss to explain—they had begun to ask for, to demand . . . things. Incredible, outrageous things that far surpassed canonical norms. Some tried going to sleep to see if their customary restraint would return by morning, but when they opened their eyes, they'd shake their wives awake and demand more. Eventually, the wives began to grant their wishes, and a new stage began. They felt like new men, as if they had shed their skins and were now different, braver creatures, bowing to no one. And now—now that they had forgotten the fears society had drummed into them—they truly began to feel lost. Nothing scared the men more than what lurked deep inside each of them. They felt as though they had been deprived of a cruel, strict goddess, and they wanted her back. It's terrifying when you realize that faith depends solely on the blood pumping inside us, on the trust that each of us chooses to place in it, rather than in set conventions. The strong and vivacious adapt well enough to this new reality, but for those who are barely able to keep their blood flowing in the best of times, well, their inner struggle is terrible to behold. With nothing left to spare, they are as feeble as weeds growing on stony ground. As these poor souls grew more sexually aroused, their inadequacies only came into starker view. For one sad night, which some of them spent utterly alone, they had mentally discarded conventional ethics but didn't have the blood to do anything about it. Blood is the only thing that reestablishes equilibrium, and only a few have it in sufficient quantity. But still, they thought, what a novelty, what an unexpected storm battering at shutters long since closed for good.

The priest was pale. He, too, was consumed by the vulgar sweats of the flesh, the sweat of a difficult night when sleep only makes things worse. An eerie light, like a child's night-light, emanated from his face. He had meekly allowed himself to be pulled into this strange new territory, the scent of which was unfamiliar, but then again his sense of smell didn't seem to be working very well anyway. He didn't know whether to breathe it in or out, but eventually found himself forced to savor the aroma. He and the terrible night-flower perfume were alone, floating in a bizarre world, with no prospect of returning to the depressing little room next to the chapel. The small, gaunt man was still growing accustomed to the semilunar twilight of sleep. But the Naked Woman was too bright for the shadows to swallow her entirely—her body glowed like mother-of-pearl on the dark seabed.

"Madam . . ." he murmured, trying to break the spell. Then she stepped forward, brighter than ever. *She is a torch of burning roses*, he thought, *but what roses! Roses that can whisper secrets, secrets that God doesn't want you to know.* She seemed to be saying in her brave, but gentle, feminine way, "It's me, I am standing before your lean face and wide forehead. It's too big for the little head you've been given. Give me that head, burning on its own like a flower in the desert. This is a night for two, give it to me."

The man suddenly saw his own head floating in the oppressive air of the room. Then it multiplied like ripples in water. But what was left of his decapitated body couldn't get ahold of any of them, as much as he chased madly around. Eventually, he picked up a butterfly net that he hadn't seen or used since childhood, and started to thrash about with it wildly. But the infernal little heads bounced about until they were well up in the sky, and from there they looked down upon him with his own eyes, regressing back into the sweet gaze of a being's first moments in life. Around, among, and against them danced thousands of transparent, overlapping colored circles.

"I just want one of my heads," the priest begged desperately, a dog howling at the moon.

The image of the woman, though faint, never faded away completely from the sea of cloned heads and circles. It was then, perhaps because of all this boisterous movement, that she started to gently rise and fall, like a fish in an aquarium. She was stylized, translucent. A continuous stream of bubbles came out of her mouth to join the heads and circles, bouncing off them or bursting in the air when they met no resistance. The man threw the net as far away as he could and stood still, watching. He had never loved a woman, or even seen the feminine form, in his life, but now both were happening, both the love and the body, and he couldn't escape it, not even if he closed his eyes. The pearly glow of the creature shone through his eyelids, growing even more lovely when filtered through his skin, like a landscape seen through water. *God, make my eyelids as strong as the walls of Jericho, don't let the trumpets tear them down. No, not yet, let them fall* . . . Finally, she came closer, damp with the sweat of their midnight dance. She didn't make a sound, not a floorboard creaked; she was a snake slithering over carpet. She hadn't said a word, and didn't now, though he had no trouble understanding her. For him, however, speech was the only option.

"I am chaste, madam, chaste and a virgin. The two things don't always coincide in a single body. They do in mine, for the glory of God, so I can't. Also, I don't want to . . ."

But this was something else that she seemed to understand: the potential of those who say they can't and the desire of those who say they won't. Suddenly, she pushed him back onto his cot, as though he had fainted, and started to squeeze him with her arms. Arms that were now very different from the ones he had seen during the dance of the circles. Now they burned like the desert sand. He was ashamed at how easily he had slipped into the embrace, his poor bones wilting before her strength. She also seemed to understand his sense of physical inferiority and stroked his ego with unsaid words: "This is the way God made things, it's the best kindling. Bones clean the air as they burn. Fat sizzles, it dirties the flames."

"But I can't," the man repeated stubbornly, as though she were asking permission. "Even if I wanted to, I would still need to be capable of it, and I'm not, I'm not!"

It was then that two terrible things happened: he was suddenly able (the gentle waves that had been lapping against his heart were rising up the beach) and the woman evaporated into thin air, horrible air that smelled like the room of a solitary priest, lacking entirely in heads, circles, or anything else of interest. The world without her . . . A gust of this different atmosphere flooded his nostrils and plunged into his still-dreaming blood, dragging him sweatily back to the surface of the morning. He heard a cock crowing in the distance. Maybe, he thought, the being that had created these dull old archetypes was about to rewrite the ancient order.

"He'll have the last word," he murmured, sitting up. "He always does."

He found his deacon in the church, praying loudly in front of an icon. Following each of the pleas that formed the leitmotif of his prayer, the man pounded hard on his chest; his frail frame seemed incapable of withstanding such punishment. Apparently he had become an armored automaton without bones to break or organs to damage.

"What's wrong, man? Why this self-abuse?" the priest asked with what little strength he possessed after his long night. "Come on, get up, we need to see to the bells, the candles, the wine. Sundays aren't to be wasted. Especially not today, I see that you've heard about this supposed woman too."

He remembered her stepping out of the shadows like a white stamen from a black flower, stroking his skin, leaving behind a delicious trail of sleep dust.

"I hate her, Father," said the deacon, standing up. His bare chest appeared unharmed by the self-flagellation.

"I heard you joined the hunt yesterday."

"I went out to look for her in the countryside, but I might as well have been chasing the devil himself. He must be the father, or son, of that naked beast. God believe me; please believe me as I must believe myself. I hate her! I hate her!"

"Do not hate so much, my son, not so much. Come on, today will be a long, strange day. As long as the dream of life itself. *Dominus dedit, Dominus abstulit, sit nomen Domini benedictum.*"

And he turned around to get something from his shoddy little room.

"Hatred," he murmured, sniffing hard, as

though he were trying to inhale a specific particle of dust. "That will be today's theme. That is what they want from me, even if they won't admit it. So we shall have hatred. My little man has never failed me before; I can always read the mood of the village in his entrails."

Just then, the bells began to ring. *Heavens, what a crazy sound*, he thought. The shrunken little creature to whom they had been entrusted since the church was built must be dangling from the rope like a hanged man trying to escape the devil. He was on his way to help him when he realized that this volume, well suited to a public calamity, was what everyone was expecting. The village's collective anxiety was being expressed as pure noise.

Having peered out at his flock in the morning light and sniffed the air, as he always did during moments of local turmoil, he saw immediately that this would be a very unusual Sunday. *It's as if the village changed its skin or was breathing a new air*, he thought as he went to the confessional. Inside the little wooden box, the confessions grew strange, strayed from their customary paths.

"Father, I can find no words to describe my sin," said the first woman to appear on the other side of the screen. "I wish I were the way I used to be. I wish I could say what I've done and wait for you to give me penitence, like we usually do. But I'm not myself and it's useless, I can't."

"Don't fret, my child. Tell me all about it," came

the reply, which was reassuring, if slightly tinged with anxiety. "You won't be the only one sharing your troubles this morning. Ever since dawn, I've sensed something strange going on. It's like I'm in a different village. You're the same people, but different too. It's as plain as the noses on your faces. But don't be afraid, unburden your troubles onto me and find relief. You won't be punished."

"No, Father," said the little woman in a tired voice. "Other women might know what to say because it's something they can talk about. My problem is different, I'm sure of that. God forgive me for my silence, but I don't know how I'd go about saying, describing things that have never happened before . . ."

A thin blast of warm air hit the priest's face. It smelled different too. Usually their breath smelled of warm milk, even if they hadn't drunk any.

"Well, it's not a question of how well you explain it. It's about feeling sinful, being aware that you have strayed from the sacred commandments, and regretting your actions deeply and unreservedly. That is the true act of contrition, although describing it here is also an obligation. Be at peace for now. This time I shall go further than I should," he said more to himself than the woman. "I shall offer absolution for an indescribable sin. Go," he commanded, his voice now back to normal. "Find what you can in prayer, which is just another form of confession."

"And after that?"

"Then go back to your children, your fields, and your everyday duties . . ."

"Everyday duties. What does that mean now? My God!"

"The duties of a humble life, my child. No more, no less. Sometimes, so I've been told by several women in this very booth, just sewing a button is enough to put one's mind at rest. The satisfaction of your husband upon seeing the button back where it should be on his shirt will help to put you at ease, even if he doesn't bother to say thank you. Words, arrows straight from God, have the divine quality of working on both great and small scales. The truly valuable ones are the most basic, the ones that serve the need to describe things. Bread and wine, for instance."

"Bread, wine," the woman repeated mechanically.

"Yes. You'll remember the names of everything served at your table today, won't you? So, let's forget the difficult words, at least until the confession that I know you'll be able to make one day. We poor sinners can't be blamed for our verbal failings."

"No, Father, I don't want your understanding. I don't want your false forgiveness, I didn't come here for that!" the women exclaimed, her whisper building into the shriek of a steam engine. "I demand that you condemn me! I need to hear you say it, it's what I deserve!"

Now she started to cry. The priest was used to postconfessional tears, as he inwardly called them. They didn't cry when they committed the sin, of course. Fat chance. Then, their tears would apparently run dry, but normal functions would resume the moment they unburdened themselves into his ear. It was as if guilt came in two stages: a personal dry spell and then a rainy season in the confessional. But this time, even the tears were unfamiliar, different than usual. Yes, he must be in a different village, he thought again, giving the woman time to cry herself out. He must have been taken to a new parish in his sleep: he was listening to bastard women confessing, not to trivial acts about which he never knew how to feel, but real, life-changing passions. Women who wanted but were unable to share the whole truth. And to top it all off, there were these new hybrid tears. This creature wasn't asking for forgiveness or succor and he was entirely unprepared.

"Good, cry for as long as you need to. Soothe those nerves."

"No," said the woman, choking down humors, mucus, and tears.

The priest heard the mixture splash into the pit of her stomach and he was feeling cruel enough to ask, "Why not? Why not allow yourself to be comforted?"

"Not even that tiny concession, my God. No charity, however small . . ."

Now it was he who chose to be silent. He was thinking of the others waiting their turn. She appeared to be talking past him to someone else, trying to use him as an intermediary. And that meant that the classic delayed confession would take shape sooner or later and the emotions would all come flooding out at once. Now she told him everything, absolutely everything, like a criminal reconstructing the scene of the crime; though torturous, it was the only way to convince them that they had really committed the act, that they were its true author.

"At first, Father, I didn't understand what he wanted. I thought that maybe he'd gone crazy and was taking advantage of that madness. I let him lead me by the nose," she said, violently blowing said nose with an insufficiently large handker-chief. "We were in bed, the house was silent, and the children were locked away. I knew something was going to happen, I could smell it in the air. He was lying on his back, his hands behind his head. I was in the same position, watchful in case he tried to strangle me or jump out the half-open window he kept looking at. He said, 'And now you must call her. Your best friend from school, the one you haven't seen for years. Everyone had a best friend, didn't they? First call her by name, then tell me what she looked like, then how she acted.' I told him everything. I felt like I was talking through a long tunnel. 'Her name was Claudine,' I answered.

'She was taller than the others; she had black hair, an olive complexion, big eyes, and wore her hair in braids. She had a husky voice, the kind of voice that people respect. She was very beautiful. One day, the teacher told us about the Amazons and we all looked at her, like we could see her on a horse with a bow and arrow . . .' 'What else?' he asked. I felt hypnotized, he was tearing it out of me piece by piece. 'If she was your best friend there must be more, secrets you shared with each other.' 'Yes,' I said stupidly. 'We went on daily outings to the woods behind the school. I had to clean the erasers and, no one ever knew, but Claudine would ask for permission to get a glass of water or do a chore or fetch something from another class.' 'And then what?' he asked, squeezing my arm urgently. 'And then we'd kiss behind a tree. It was so long ago. Please stop torturing me,' I begged, moving away from him, to the edge of the bed. That was when he wrapped his fingers around my neck and, in a voice I'd never heard before, said, 'Now you're going to repeat her name, once, twice, a hundred times, until you're sure she's back. Then all the other things you're keeping to yourself are going to happen again. She will be here, between the two of us, completely naked like that bitch sniffing around the fields today.'"

"Christ Almighty," murmured the priest, trying to gauge the scope of the sin.

"No, Father, I haven't finished yet. I began to

call her with his awful fingers still clamped around my throat. I don't know how many times I said her name. I remembered how the eraser fell from my hands . . . Claudine's breasts weren't small like the others, her chest was pert under her blouse and her heart was beating like a hammer. He started to loosen his fingers and I began to lose myself, to let the naked wanderer—I could see her face now—fly in like a ghost through the window. She bonded with us in ways I never knew existed, ways that I never knew I was capable of. The devil may have been pulling our cart of madness, but I was the one cracking the whip."

"My child," the priest said vaguely, like someone who has been punched in the nose and doesn't know whether to hit back or tend to his wound.

"Yes, Father, it happened just like I said. But he'll never know, not really. I'll never tell him. I'll always do what I did last night, spit at him, scratch him, but inside I was screaming with joy, dragging us further and further down until we lost consciousness. The desire will creep back into its shameful shadows, just like before. But I will be desperate to experience it again. I don't know what to call it, it's a sin of a thousand forms, but it makes you forget about heaven every night. My God. I'll be longing for the night to last six months, like it does in other parts of the world."

"What does heaven have to do with it?"

"Because heaven is heaven. The other place has

no name, but it comes before heaven. And then, when you look out the window in the morning, the sky seems limited, too dull, blue, and even."

There was nothing left to do but face facts. A key word had lost its power. The woman felt weak, anemic, after her revelation. If she died then and there before her confession had finished, she thought, she'd be taken away with her hands crossed over her chest and her head covered in a white veil, as was customary for last rites. But the injustice of Claudine's death—twenty years forgotten was the same as death—would buzz around her like the first posthumous fly, stripping the spectacle of its dignity like an unkempt interloper at a lavish funeral.

The priest, sensing that she was lost in her memories, allowed them to run their natural course. What was there for him to say? His head was spinning. He knew very well that he wasn't up to the job. He had become a priest as casually as other people decide to be tailors, doctors, or carpenters. His mother had promised him to the priesthood if he recovered from tuberculosis after being sent away to the mountains. He would never know whether it was divine influence or just the fresh mountain air that had saved him, but he accepted his fait accompli. *This is what mothers of a single child are*, he thought, *female leviathans whose monstrous love lines the coat of the devil himself.* At the time, he had had an interest in painting, but he threw away his brushes and took the sacred vows. Now that his mother was dead and God was more or less mummified inside of him, this crisis was a test to be overcome. The worst part was that even before the Naked Woman—suddenly her image lit up the air like a lamp—his brushes had come back, as though the hangman had followed his victim into limbo. He observed people with the eyes of the trade, paying more attention to their colors and shapes than their problems. Sometimes he had to drag himself out from among the golden flecks that sparkled in certain eyes as they begged him for the absolution he was forgetting to administer. But he had to keep going. He must get rid of this sinner and shorten the sessions with the ones that would follow. He would allow himself to be punished by the words that would come raining down upon him and endeavor to mete out a little punishment himself. Otherwise his flock would think that he wasn't doing his job.

Just then, the twins arrived at the church, still shaking off the water that had been thrown over them. The bruises on their faces and mussed-up hair, like that of newly hatched chicks, bore evidence of what they had been up to. One of the men who had helped get them to church provided a whispered explanation to an inquisitive old lady.

"It seems, so the slightly less stupid one told me, that he woke up on the straw in the barn where they've been sleeping since they were orphans and tried to wake the other one as usual. But this time he couldn't."

"Was he sick? God help the poor little things," said the old woman, crossing herself.

"No, of course not. He was dreaming, you see. Dreaming of the . . . well, you know, the woman they met in the field."

"You can dream of anything, God help us. Then He comes and erases it from your mind with a swipe of His finger."

"But it seems that when his brother finally managed to shake him awake, the boy was upset. He didn't want to be shaken out of this particular dream. Or at least that's what it sounded like from what he was mumbling when he attacked his brother: 'I'll kill you. I'll smash your face in, you thief. You want her for yourself, don't you? But I saw her first, she's mine. I'll crush you like a spider in the straw.'"

The man providing the account had gone into the barn to fetch some fodder and found them rolling around at each other's throats. Like a pair of scrapping dogs, the only thing that could separate them was a bucket of water.

The old woman knelt down on a pew. For a moment it looked as though she were going to faint, but then she could be heard praying rapidly.

"Save them, my God, save them from the clutches of the pale demon who knows how to slip into people's dreams . . ."

"In the beginning, God created heaven and earth. The earth was a void filled with mist. Only the spirit of God moved over the waters . . ." the priest began, ascending to the pulpit, though it was still too soon after the stories that had been spreading throughout the congregation for them to pay much attention to the impersonal realms of Genesis.

After these words, apparently uttered as a prelude to something, there was a lengthy silence. The congregation was used to these lapses. They saw them as the mental deficiency of a poor public speaker, a fault they forgave in return for the many debts they racked up during confession. Even though they were so lacking in God's grace, he generously tended to their humble needs, which were now expressing themselves physically (but not uncomfortably: they could cough, clear their throats, and shuffle around; their minds might even wander a little). Suddenly, the priest snapped out of his meditative trance. He always came back changed and squinting, his face paler, as if the anxiety that had taken hold had sapped his strength.

Calmer now, either because the pause had done him good or for more mysterious reasons, he repeated the introduction, building the great frieze of the Old Testament in his head. He began with the lack of color, the black at the beginning of the myth, the empty, formless earth. The void. And then the spirit spreading massively across the water. Color did not yet exist, there was no color to liven things up. But he had to use one, at least, to conceive and define the painting inside of him. Should he beg the indulgence of these people and ask them how? A terrible idea. Only God, stained from His belly to His ears by His many aborted attempts at the universal canvas, would be able to understand him. He settled on a color for the spirit floating across the water, but as yet that color was formless. He needed to come up with a form, but he had nothing for reference, nothing like it had come before . . . Enough. He knew exactly how long they were willing to put up with his pauses; he had them on an auditory leash.

"And on the first day, God said: Let there be light, and there was. And God saw that it was good. And He split the darkness. He called the light day and the darkness night . . ."

Now it was a round fruit, half shadow, half light, an extremely thin plane splitting the two. The air of those first days was saturated with miasma, but the shift toward geometry was promising. *Light and shadow make everything possible*—he thought, almost smiling at the revelation—*form, color, scale*. But what was his congregation thinking about? A vision of the collective imagination passed before his eyes. He saw the Naked Woman from his dream run into the first day, reveling in the light like a fish in water. He needed to get control of his sermon before it was too late. But the premature mother-of-pearl that he'd accidentally begun to squeeze over the landscape before the sea had been created continued to flow.

"On the second day, God said: Let there be a firmament across the waters to separate them. And thus the sky was made. And on the third day, He said: Let the waters under the sky withdraw to create the arid and the dry. And thus the land and the sea were created. And it was good. God saw that it was good, says Scripture. And then He said: Let there be green grass and fruiting plants and seeds . . ."

The green of the first giants—the color was more important than the form—an abstract green, the green of creation, one of God's great wonders. What an enchanting revelation. He then had an idea, both clean and morbid, the two poles between which his life was always torn. His victory lay in the middle, where neither held sway. He could just leave. Abandon the villagers as they stared open-mouthed, as though he had vanished into thin air. Then he, too, could join the search for the Naked Woman; he would leave no stone unturned, would find her lying unconscious on the ground and revive her with a kiss. The two of them would set out on an exhilarating flight, running free on the trail of a long-lost legend. "Where shall we go?" she'd ask suddenly, panting beneath her Madonna hair. And he would tell her that he had just discovered an ancient color, the oldest in the world, that he wanted to paint her in front of such a powerful backdrop, chaste and naked just as she was, with her shapely legs, flat primitive feet, and belly large enough to give birth to stars. Yes, exactly like that, much as she might laugh. God always to the fore, creating more and more days, and they running madly, obsessively back through time, to the first divine verdure trodden by the first woman in the world, contradicting God and Scripture alike . . .

"On the fourth day," he went on somewhat reluctantly, fighting back a yawn at everything that had been created thus far, "there were lights in the sky to distinguish day from night and to mark time. On the fifth day, there were reptiles in the water and birds flying over the earth and under the firmament of the sky. And on the sixth day, God said: Let there be living animals of every kind, domestic animals and wild beasts across the earth . . ."

A disingenuous thought came to him, that perhaps he held the course of history in his hands. He even seemed to be providing a decent interpretation of the bearded, monotonous voice of the Bible.

"And on that sixth day, He saw that, as everything He had done was good, He must invent man in his own likeness and image, to take charge of everything that moves and lives, which He had created on the earth and under the sky. And so on the sixth day, God created man . . ."

Once again the sin of silence, but there was nothing for it. God was lost in the depths of His thoughts, in the immense task of manifesting, organizing, and anticipating the succession of his creatures. Back then, only the lovely form of Adam existed, wandering around naked and sad among the trees. The priest could see his innocent legs, still stumbling around clumsily, yet to find their feet. He thought about how difficult it had always been, artistically speaking, to depict a man who is not yet a man, especially when he symbolized the entire species that would sprout forth from between those pure thighs. And it was even harder to conceive of his sadness, the first sadness of the world. Was Adam happy and free? How could he be? He had been forbidden something. It was the first thing to be denied to man, but more would follow, right down to the insignificant, slack-jawed descendants in his congregation, all of whom were so blinkered and in denial about their urges. Except for him, of course. He was on his own, a village priest, ranged against God and His pitiable creations, with a long-haired woman standing next to him, waiting to be painted against a newborn green backdrop.

"The Lord had planted a garden of delights," he went on dreamily, "and there He placed the man whom He had shaped from the clay of the earth and brought to life with the breath of the Holy Spirit. He put him there and told him to guard and cultivate His paradise and eat the fruit of the trees, except for one that He picked out especially. But God could see that this wasn't working. He, Himself alone, my beloved children, must have understood that complete solitude can only be withstood by God Almighty. And so then He said: Let us give company to this complex individual who has no peer among the birds of the air or the beasts of the earth. And that was when the dream of man occurred, in accordance with divine thought. While the first man was asleep, God removed a bone from his flesh to create a woman, and left this woman for the man to find when he woke up . . ."

Here, as usual, there was a brief pause. The relief was palpable.

"The woman was naked, of course, naked in her purity and innocence, and the man was naked and pure as well," added the priest, in a slightly more judgmental voice.

There was a sharp, collective intake of breath— nudity had been invoked. This was why they had come. They didn't give a damn about the first couple, though admittedly they had been led along by the tale like children listening to a familiar story, unwilling to put up with even minor variations to the plot. But now an unclothed woman had been named, and it didn't matter who it was. Everyone hoped that the priest would just shut up so they could deal with the issue in their own way. But this time their mental urging failed and the voice went on unperturbed.

"God had called upon Adam to name all the beasts of the earth and birds of the sky, and choose one of them to keep him company. But after giving each their own name, he rejected them all. Then, upon waking, still half asleep, he saw among trees that still dripped a dark, primitive green, a shape that was alike but not his own, a skin that was his skin but different, a shadow, also both the same and different, seeking out his own . . ."

Then suddenly the priest plunged back into his old pit of silence, leaving them to their own devices once more. But he continued inwardly like a man possessed. Desire, the delightful possibilities of contact, did not yet exist. So pure, abstract, beauty must have reigned. Because love and its sinful echo did not yet exist, they were just naked, ignorant bodies newly born of the fire of God like a pair of unique ceramics. How could they be painted when even the great Michelangelo used models that had already been compromised by an event as yet unknown to the freshly forged air?

"And so, my dear children," he went on, to his listeners' surprise. "As you know, as you've heard many times: both the man and the woman were naked and they felt no embarrassment or shame at their state. But the serpent tempted the woman to eat the fruit of the tree. And she succumbed and tempted her partner. And as soon as they had both eaten, they felt as though their eyes had been opened—*Eritis sicut dei*. And they saw what they had never seen before: their primitive nudity. And so they covered themselves with leaves. And then, feeling even more ashamed, they hid from God behind some trees, and explained their shame from there."

It was inevitable. The speaker had to abandon his lyrical tone at some point. They all anticipated the move, so much so that they were now waiting for one of his signature gestures, the ceremonial casting away of an apple core. But they were desperately hoping that it wouldn't happen. They would have been able to stand the entire Bible, from Genesis to Revelation, so long as he didn't address the issue head on. They cherished the pale, curvy subject they were keeping aloft with bated breath, afraid that if it were brought down to earth it would be lost.

"Oh, I know," the priest went on in a nonchalant tone, as though he were just another member of the congregation. He hadn't yet thrown away the core. "You've been browbeaten with the story of lost innocence for some time. Books and men of God have been repeating it in different ways for so long that it has become nothing more than a fairy tale. Woman, as you know, was punished with the pain of childbirth and man with the sweat he would have to shed over the earth to make it bear fruit. And is that it?

you say. Eve—life, that is—and Adam were thrown out of paradise. So, you ask again, is that everything for today?"

But suddenly he threw the core far away and the wretch's artificial tone cracked. An irritable force had been building in his deceptively weak breast, the same breast that had recovered in the mountains and in so doing was condemned to abstinence by binding contract. "That story has been repeated over and over again," he shouted suddenly. "Is original sin an old story? No, a thousand times no." What did they think the river in which they had been splashing around consisted of? He had shown them its source, but only from downstream. And it had borne them pitilessly to their present horror, dragging them into the ancient swamp where they now found themselves. Not even his familiar hacking cough could compete with the power of his admonitions. Yes, they had been sullying their pure inheritance, the bread of life, with sinful thoughts, he told them bitterly. They didn't care whether the cow went thirsty over the course of the long day or whether the haphazardly drawn milk was spilt, they were playing fast and loose with the livelihood of their children and the good of the village. Furrows were left unploughed, the cheese uncurdled, and the butter was melting in the sun. Grace could scarcely be heard at the table.

The bread and wine were flavorless, wolfed

down to gain time for something else. Of course: the villagers needed to find someone, to bring her to justice. But they were acting on nothing more than the twins' dubious eye-witness account. And no one, not the sheriff, the priest, nor anyone else, had been consulted about their activities over the past feverish day and long, dirty night.

The priest left them to muse on this for a minute or two, their shoulders hunched and ears burning. This respite, he thought, would be one of the last. A few more acts and he'd have unmasked them completely.

"No one has asked this of you," he continued, "because the woman does not and has never existed. At least not for anyone who is not as clean as she. She exists only for those who are worthy of touching her. Which is to say that she does not exist at all. Yes, don't make those worried faces on my account, I haven't gone mad. Eve, as I explained to you, was thrown out of paradise because of the fruit. But wherefore all this shame and fear of the eye of God with its clear waters and fathomless beauty? That, as strange as it may seem, is what I ask you today. She has returned, that is all. Because she now knows that God wanted her to eat the fruit. The Naked Woman is passing through the village, seeking to appeal her judgment. And she mocks you and your poor feminine other halves, you who are so primly attired but incapable of eternal love. Oh, she is more than a woman, and she may well dazzle us with her game, but what is the point of trying to share the scent of this rose, the first flesh rose to walk the earth, with the likes of you?"

The priest's last words were smothered in a wave of coughing and creaking joints. But not his poetry, which remained suspended in the air like a trapeze artist over a safety net. For the first time, she, the woman, had been mentioned and named. She was initially linked to biblical myth, then hell in a manner bordering on heresy. Now she could be seen in thousands of different forms, depending on the image each carried inside of them. Her shape had been as vague as a sliver of the moon in the daylight, but no longer. Given form by the priest's words, and what words they were, the femme fatale hardened in each of the incarnations of her spell, bathing them in the breath of truth, perfuming their faces with her hair, scratching every palm with her nails.

The priest, meanwhile, had paused once again, ostensibly to clear his throat. But as he pretended to be lost in thought, he surveyed the congregation and gauged their reaction.

"I say she does not exist," he repeated, his voice taking on a prophetic timbre.

He looked over toward where the twins usually sat. A sunbeam shone through a small window high up on the wall, close to the ceiling. Refracted by the glass, it fell on one of the boy's faces, making it impossible to see. *Who knows what this solar phenomenon might signify?* he thought. Perhaps it was accusing him of being an apostate. Or maybe the accusation was being leveled at the boy, who wouldn't know where to begin defending himself. There was no doubt that it had fallen on one of the most inexpressive faces in the village.

"But even if she were to appear here now, she would still not exist. Not for the feeble minds of her discoverers, at least . . . *Stultorum infinitus est numerus*," he declared, admiring Solomon, the king who was always one step ahead, and blessing the fact that the Bible was written in Latin.

All heads turned toward the twins, both of whom were now bathed in the diffuse light. The priest was stunned for a moment, for this really did seem like some kind of sign. But fortunately he, an aficionado of color, was the only one to notice.

"Yes," he added, bellowing to attract attention back to himself, "even if she does not exist for those who are unworthy of her, I shall continue my admonishment: Let he who did not sin in the shadow of paradise last night cast the first stone."

He saw a cloud of unease fall upon each and every one of them.

"It is *you*, then, who are the dirty, naked ones—not her. And now unblock your ears, hear this, I have saved this news for the end. When our village has long since disappeared, as perhaps the heavens have ordained, this truth shall continue to float above the ashes like a winged creature: I, too, dreamed last night. I"—he repeated, beating his chest—"sinned wonderfully in my dream of her. And I do not ask forgiveness of God, my flock, or anyone else. This is the difference between you and me: you spit her out once you've had your way with her, even though you're left wanting more, while I condemn myself on her behalf. And that is all for the day. Leave. *Qui habet aures audiendi audiat.*"

The little man in the pulpit had tested every limit imaginable: his courage, his voice, and the patience of his audience. He had already been flashed several fiery gazes and tempers seemed very close to boiling over when, in the last row of pews, a woman let out a bestial howl of pain that sounded like it came from the very bowels of the earth. First everyone froze, then the entire congregation ran to her aid. The priest slowly descended from his pulpit, patting at his sweaty forehead with a drenched handkerchief.

"Disgusting woman," he murmured, "coming into the house of God to give birth. But nonetheless, John, I am grateful," he said, stopping before the image of the church's patron saint. "You've distracted the rabble . . ."

He had no interest in finding out what they were going to do about the birth or whatever the commotion was. He left through the small side door that led to the vestry. His desertion did not indicate indifference, he told himself perfectly reasonably, but was rather a result of what he had said from the pulpit. His words still scorched the air. If he bore any of the blame for what was happening, neither his help nor his presence would be appropriate. Better to leave them to their own devices. At least the barbaric pain they were about to witness would serve as a warning. It was a chapter from the ancient story they'd just heard. And God was rubbing it in their faces, presenting them with a woman split in two. He had clearly grown tired of mere suggestion.

He looked through the crumbling blinds, inhaling their scent with pleasure, and saw that the crowd had begun to break up, perhaps to make room for the more capable among them to do their work. He pictured them in his mind, wrinkled like apples over hot coals. But also with a mortal lump, something had shriveled inside of them, allowing their hatred to show. Yes, he had been sure of it from the moment early that morning when he had heard his deacon beating himself on the chest. Then, as he had let loose his sermon like a hailstorm, as each of them envisaged their punishment over eternal flames, the woman they wanted became more real, more intimate, and even more urgent. *But there must be more to it,* he thought, *even if most of them are unaware.* They were too brutish to fully understand their disgust with themselves, the nauseating sensation they had been feeling since the day before, and the only way they knew to express it was through hatred. They hated the unknown, they hated other people, and they hated themselves. The woman had shown each of them who they truly were, and it wasn't the kind of revelation that was easily forgiven, at least while there was something still wriggling under the stone. She was free in her nudity, there could be no argument about that. But this demonstration of individual freedom only made their own plight starker. For example, the person who had neglected to wash their feet before they put on their shoes would feel the grit of manure between their toes and be ashamed in a way that had never occurred to them before. Another might worry about a vestigial tail. But minor details like these were just the start; there were much larger flaws that had long been carefully dressed up like a donkey at the fair. But even ribbons can chafe a wound, and so their shared revelations left them with no choice but to reject both the woman and each other. A single incarnation of freedom cannot exist without starting a war, perhaps because the splendor of its devotion is too great. How could they not condemn a nudity that reminded them so powerfully of their own imperfections? And wallowing in their disillusionment was as much as they were capable of, he concluded, still looking at them.

Meanwhile, he continued to detect the scent of sun-warmed wood in everything, whether oozing droplets of retained sap, or just the embalmed memory of its past. *At least this*, he thought, stroking the wood as though it were still alive, *the stuff from which the village was made, never gets distracted by the latest scandal. It remains upright, in perfect equilibrium with itself and won't ever get upset about anything.* One of these days, if God or the village didn't bring him to judgment first, he would take up their Sunday with a speech about wood: how it dies without rotting, meaning that it, in fact, lives on. Then there was that man, whose name he'd forgotten, the one who sat on a stone to take off his shoes and built himself a log cabin. One spring day, his eyes popping out of his skull in wonder, he saw that the logs, which had been sawed up and ruthlessly chained together, were sprouting once more. "Before they die for good next summer," he had explained in passing, sure that the priest wouldn't be satisfied with such a simplistic notion but tickled nonetheless by the captive branches. The priest told himself that he'd have to make it into a parable. The forest does not rot, not even the forest of the dead, whose roots delve deep into wormy tombs. But those who plant them do indeed rot, sometimes before they're even dead, and this can have unfortunate atmospheric consequences for their neighbors. But what about him? He was just another pawn of time, he told himself objectively, and just as susceptible to mass decomposition. But he was without God and without fear. He lacked all the things that his fellow man had invented to protect himself: that was the difference. A man absolutely on his own. So, what could he use for self-defense if not the trees that had been rooted deep in the earth to prop up the heavens? At that moment he became entirely convinced that all this was truly happening. Even as he tried to persuade others that appearances could be deceptive, the alluring, fleshy reality of the evasive woman grew more and more tangible as she lay down upon the primordial greenery he had recently discovered, taking his brush out of his hand, wetting it with her own saliva to lighten the tone, and handing it back to him with her large palms. And that was when she no longer fit the unworthy canvas he had stretched out for her. Neither did she fit on the surface of his earth of green monsters. She remained in the dome of the sky. He would be forced to rely on the grace of God to create this immense fresco, whose innate fleshy roses would exceed all expectations.

"Even the humble amateur painter, Lord, awed and cowed before this beauty that has escaped Your hands, falls from Your scaffolding, and returns to the mortal condition to which the rest of Your creatures are subject," he said suddenly with the honesty of someone who has already embarked upon their descent into damnation. "But not even there," he murmured, expending the last of his mental strength, "can one feel free of the model, the shifting figure in the night, not in her role as Madonna in her dome, but ready for the embrace that is the source of all man's agony. The agony of a man desperately seeking an earthly partner to help assuage his fear . . ."

This harrowing confession, not dissimilar to those of many who had thrown themselves at his feet that morning, begging for judgment, left him disoriented for several minutes. He had shattered into little pieces, each of which seemed to contain some aspect of his character. However, because they lacked the false support of the whole, none of the minister of God, the artist, the slave to his mother, or the man hungry for love were able to find purchase independently of one another.

"And yet," he said from his innermost being as he paced the room, his hands tucked into his sleeves, "we must make a categorical choice and leap into the abyss even if it means our disgrace." Anything was better than the interregnum ruled by God, or his opposite number, in which he was thrashing around. Much as it pained him to admit, he was no different from his flock. Like them, he had dreamed and he had spoken of it afterward, a sin for which the will of God was only potentially a mitigating factor. The Almighty could hardly go about tightening His system to condemn dreams now, but perhaps in the darkness He had left the keys to the room to which we are all called sooner or later. Even the purity of the chosen few deserves a little leeway from time to time. But the worst possibility, the one that would bring down the greatest wrath from the never-sleeping eye, was that she had actually come to him on real feet, the kind that walk, feel pain, and enjoy being rubbed. He, too, had left his door ajar, not daring to lock the church as he did every night. And she could well have been there, howling her damning, gentle exceptionality up at the stained-glass windows like a white wolf.

"Enough, by God, enough!" he shouted suddenly, lowering a cloth over the peephole as though to bury himself in his own solitude, or self-annihilation. He fell to his knees. "*In manus tuas, Domine, in manus tuas . . .*"

☾

"Look, look over there!" exclaimed the wife of the crime novel aficionado, standing up in the crowd having lunch outside.

Her eyes and mouth were open as wide as they could go, providing both a fair reflection of her anxiety and an ample view of her half-chewed food.

"What? What do you see? Speak!" shouted her husband, anxious to add a new discovery to that of the fingernail.

"Nothing, I'm sorry," she said eventually, swallowing with difficulty. "I thought I saw someone in the distance, next to the rails. But then I remembered the haystack set alight by sparks from the train . . . Unless I've caught your fever," she added ironically. "Those novels make you look for clues all over the place."

The man stared at her hard, as if he were trying to wring out a message she wanted to keep to herself.

"Give me that apple, don't cut it," he said, returning to the age-old obsession.

"What about it? What could you possibly have seen in it? I picked it this morning from our tree. The others are over there in that bag," she replied, sitting back down.

"Look at it," he said mysteriously, aware of the audience forming around him. "Don't these marks look like they might've been made by teeth? If so, it could prove that she spent the night hiding in one of our gardens. The search should recommence today, but in reverse, from under our beds and outward."

"Or from our wisdom teeth to the children's milk teeth," someone said, testing the potential for humor in the affair, as he passed exhibit A to his neighbor with a nudge.

"I have a goat that's in the habit of taking bites out of the forbidden fruit," said another.

"It can easily be determined," said the aficionado, ignoring the gibes. "Every person's dental imprint is different. And just by sight, with no need for further examination, reproduction, or comparison. You can measure the space between each tooth and study the marks left by the palate, or the gum indentations if it happens to be a soft fruit."

As in his initial demonstration of his expertise, when he had found the nail, he was just about to win back his prestige. Instead, however, as the apple continued on its rounds he tried to turn the joke back on those who had made fun of him.

"Although on this occasion I was immediately able to observe that the marks were not left by teeth at all but rather the indentation imprinted by barbed wire upon the growing fruit. Had they been made by teeth, the space between the incisors would have indicated an enormous mouth."

They looked at him in astonishment. This incomprehensible language was something that must be respected even if they did not quite understand it.

"So, they weren't teeth at all, thank goodness," said the last woman to whom the apple arrived. "But I still don't think it should be eaten, she might have poisoned it from afar with her breath."

She: she had borne this name for several hours now, perhaps thanks to the veil of absolution that the priest had draped over her body in his role as public defender. Dressed like that, in just her essential femininity, she could be given a better name and her deeds didn't seem so heinous. Of course, it was some leap from there to believing that she didn't exist, as the sermon had argued. But the general uncertainty over her physical presence only confused the issue of pollution and biological warfare in the women's fevered minds.

"I think that we should start boiling our water too; she must have had a drink somewhere before vanishing into thin air."

"*Psst* . . . they're talking about the naked lady," hissed a young freckled boy to his albino friend. "She's driven them all crazy. But guess what: she doesn't want to mess with anyone, just me."

"What?"

They were forbidden from talking about it, the subject being reserved for grown-ups, but it was in their imagination, the true vessel and oral conveyance of myth, that the episode would take on really adventurous, hallucinatory proportions.

"Yes, lash freak, you heard: just me. Don't you get mad too, or you'll try and scratch out my eyes like you do when I show you how I can look at the sun without closing them."

"I'm not mad. I know you're lying about you and the woman. Liar."

"Liar? If only you could've seen her . . . She came to my bed last night on tiptoe and touched my head with a green branch she had in her hand. She said that one day, when I had grown up, we'd get married in this church right here."

"Naked?" his friend asked, looking at the building as though he were expecting the procession to emerge at any moment.

"Yes, naked, but in a dress made of water with a transparent flower in her hair."

"Would the dress have a train?" the albino asked.

"Of course. A long train that leads all the way back to the river. Carried by two huge snails," the freckled boy said, keeping his eyes fixed on the apple. Any moment now it was going to be tossed away as though it carried the plague.

"Lies, lies, and more lies!" barked the boy with the pink irises. "She's going to marry my big brother, not you. She likes cars that start with a whisper, with soft, feathery seats. And hot and cold air. And music, and even an ash tray."

"And did you see them together, pink eye, or is that just what he told you?"

"Both. My brother told me when he came to visit us for Christmas. He brought me a toy, one with a sticker and everything."

"Mine!" the freckled boy screamed, pouncing on the apple that had just been thrown to the ground.

The pale boy sprang on top of him.

"Boys, in the name of God, be careful! I didn't mean to throw it to you!"

The boy was losing his baby teeth, but this didn't prevent him from taking a hearty bite. The risk of a spanking was nothing compared to his determination to lose his innocence.

"They won't eat them at home," said his mother, looking miserably at the fruit. "They must have heard about the marks. But why?"

The boy's naïveté only enhanced the strange

atmosphere. Suddenly, people began to burst out laughing, the wave of hilarity spreading through each family in turn. Everyone laughed in their own way: some grabbed their bellies, others showered their neighbors in saliva, while others almost wet themselves.

"See?" the freckled boy said with the last seed still in his mouth, resuming their argument. "She still has the branch she touched me with. Now she's tickling the soles of my feet, but no one can see her. Last night my mom and dad spent hours giggling under the sheets. They started up after she left my room. Did you hear anything?"

The pale boy had nothing to compare with his adversary's account. In addition to having to hear about his romance with the transparent woman, now he had to put up with the sight of him wolfing down the apple without sharing.

"Nothing to say?" the freckled boy taunted, picking pieces of fruit from between his teeth.

Humiliation and impotence were eating away at the albino boy in the usual way, but now they were exacerbated by other, more subtle factors. Not only was he different from the others in that he was vulnerable to sunlight, but he had been dim-witted enough to sleep through an electric night like the one just past, when an incandescent fairy had been on the loose. His image of her was shaped by his own fantasies, with all the freedoms afforded by such an existence.

"No, nothing!" he said, like a little milk-fed demon. "But take this, and this, and this . . ." He bit into the other boy's earlobe, buried his knee in his stomach, and scratched wherever he could: each "this" diligently inflicted by a white tomcat with no hope of finding love on this green earth.

They had to be separated in the same way as the twins: with a bucket of water over their heads. Then the women began to gather their things. They needed to get back: they had left their men alone in their vulnerable homes.

☾

The Naked Woman finally arrived at the edge of the thicket. Now she could see the village beyond the milking sheds and backyards. Her hair got tangled in the last defensive line of thorns: a bush that seemed to have appeared out of nowhere. "They don't want me to leave just yet," she reassured herself. "After all the trouble they've gone to in revealing their secrets to me, they'd suckle me for the rest of their lives on their tart, bitter juices. Two or three more days and I'd become one of them, a degree of intimacy that it would take me years to achieve in a normal relationship. But why remember when it's always better to forget . . ."

She shook herself free, leaving several parts of herself behind in the branches and taking some of the bushes with her. She walked on, but the grass in the clearing burned her feet. It had been basking in the sun and although it had looked soft from afar, it turned out to be rough and full of sharp little spines that pricked her already tender skin.

Yet again, she ignored her physical discomfort. She had come to find something, something hard to describe, she mentally explained to the little monsters digging into her flesh—stones, thorns, and stingers—something that didn't appear to have an entry in the well-ordered columns of the dictionary. She would never be able to say that she had found it, or at least not, "I have it, its name is . . ." But she sensed inside of her that it was alive and would release a power sufficient for escape, for rupture. To get away, it didn't matter where, to break the chains that others brandish like a beggar exhibiting his wounds. *No small matter, don't you think? I'm like someone searching for a bird that never existed even though they can hear it singing every day. On their day off, they pick up their cage and sun hat and say goodbye to the domestic world for a few hours. But then they don't come back. "Why don't they return?" everything they have left behind asks for a while. But the solitary person knows. They know their worth because they have experienced many things they had never known before, each with its own banner, showing its true colors rather than the faded standards of the dead.*

It was thus significant that in exchange for her adventure, all she felt was pain in her feet, tangles in her hair, and her stomach rumbling with its infuriating hunger. *The bonds of emotion dig far deeper, tying you in knots until the very last: the moment when you would give anything for a little more air in your nostrils, only now the oxygen doesn't deign to enter, passing you by like a friend it no longer has any use for.*

So she continued to drop breadcrumbs to mark her path, like in the fairy tale, and these tidbits wouldn't be gobbled up by the birds. She was a little worried, however, that the hunger of her empty belly would ruin everything. Her freedom, as everyone who has had to fight tooth and nail to achieve it knows, was bread enough for her teeth. Teeth that had so often been met with only iron or air but that were now sunk into an indivisible dough, a batch that had risen to smother its creators.

Eventually she realized that she was sneaking up to the rear of one of the houses. She crossed the path that ran behind it and placed her hand on a pinwheel standing by the entrance. Suddenly the world was in her hands. The spell that had come over the village had arranged for a pail of milk to be left unattended as compensation for her return from the forest.

"Milk . . . so this is how I am met on my return. A substance that man has never fully understood," she said in a quiet voice, looking around warily. "A blood-like substance with a deceptive color . . ."

She was about to pick up the milk pail when she was distracted by an unexpected new revelation in the form of short, sharp barks; these minor epiphanies appeared to be occurring in a preestablished order.

"No . . . no . . ." she said in a soothing tone, trying to muffle the sound with both hands.

She was facing an enormous gray animal with bluish-white spots spread across its cloudy belly. A stormy morning sky, wavering between sun and rain, she ventured poetically. But the situation called for submission. The animal showed that it knew its role: it sat on its hind legs, its back to the door, facing the enemy, in full control of its territory. Of course, she couldn't conceal her soft underbelly, studded with pink teats.

"Oh," exclaimed the woman, who crouched down when she saw them. "So that's your secret?"

She started to stroke the dog's head, ears, and neck, then her mammary glands as the soft underbelly was left exposed to indicate surrender. The dog instinctively forgot her mistrust. This unspoken communication with the female wanderer accelerated the process. Used to having to choose between fight or flight, the woman's peaceful approach, which seemed entirely genuine, had caught the animal off guard, and now she allowed herself to enjoy the sensation, reveling in the sensuous rubbing. Every now and again she whined in pleasure.

"If I'd seen you earlier, I'd have known that you were Grisalba," said the woman, still stroking the dog. "But better late than never, don't you agree? And you would end up forgetting everything that came before, even the name they gave you with the same lack of imagination with which they name their houses . . . Have you noticed? Yes, of course you have. The whole family puts their heads together for weeks trying to come up with a name, and then they settle on one seen a hundred times before: something like 'The Refuge.' But the promised rest is just a mirage: they have to prune the trees, rake the leaves, and argue from dawn till dusk like every other boring couple . . ."

The abandoned milk pail was close by, and the animal watched as the woman stretched out an arm to pick it up and bring it to her lips. As she drank, the milk cascaded down the sides of her face. She stopped every now and again to inspect the contents of the pail, as though to make certain of her find, before raising it again with a smile that was becoming increasingly human in spite of all her wounds.

"Grisalba," she said eventually, holding the pail to her chest. "I know. Believe it or not, I can see it in here. Suddenly, as often happens with such magical waters, the scene appeared before my eyes, in great detail. You will betray me, that is how I interpret the images, but they're fading now. In spite of our sudden love and the fact that you have allowed me to stroke your teats, you'll bark as soon as I try to leave the house, won't you? Won't you? Isn't that what you're thinking? But listen: stay with me at least until the haystack. I want a little shade before I'm killed."

She put down the pail and stood up. The dog got up too and walked along with her a little way.

"What if I try to escape? What if I do escape?" she said optimistically.

But as soon as the woman made a move, the animal's generosity disappeared. She started to bark as passionately as she could, putting all her effort into it. For a second of suspense, her gaze stayed fixed on the stranger, whose outline and sorry physical state stood out starkly against the yellow hay. The woman lost herself in the depths of ageless eyes, which were violet and narrowed into a teary, reddish corner. They were different and yet reminiscent of those of the horse, she thought. Within them you could see the origins of all free animals, distorted by many years of subservience.

Another slight shift of her foot and the dog barked some more. This time the woman was reminded of the many different forms of hysteria. When silence fell again, she noticed that something had changed. She could no longer hear the monotonous sound of a milk churner in a nearby shed. It was during this pause that a man appeared in the doorway. The afternoon sun shone a rectangle onto the wood behind him. It was a poorly proportioned frame, he barely fit inside it, but his naked, bread-crust torso gleamed under his reddish hair. At first, he didn't seem to notice the barking. He calmly went back inside and the rumbling of the machine resumed. Then he came back out into the open air and headed toward the haystack. The dog, covering the distance in little leaps, ran around him in perfect circles, careful not to trip him up, and then loped off to where she had left her living prey, who was standing still, as if hypnotized. The woman stood in front of the cone-shaped haystack with one arm across her chest, holding her shoulder in a fragile, defensive pose that accentuated her wounded appearance.

The man was entirely unprepared for the shock. He swayed in the air as though he had tripped on something. Then he felt his face freeze into a mask of stupidity. It seemed that the slightest gust of air would send him tipping over next to his dog.

"You . . . here . . . in my house . . ." he stammered eventually. "You . . . completely . . ."

They didn't take their eyes off one another. Apparently they were finding it hard to express their situation in words.

"Yes, it's me," the woman said finally in a dark, sweet voice that was just as velvety as her gaze.

She understood everything. He seemed to be endeavoring to provide a clumsy account of recent events, of which she had apparently been the cause, but he couldn't quite get his head around it.

"But is it really you? I can't believe it."

"They've been looking for me, haven't they?" she asked in turn, as if speaking to an idiot, which is what the circumstances seemed to require.

"Yes," he said. "Me too, I was with them."

"Why is that? Tell me."

The man looked resentful. He closed his eyes, striving to erase all memory of his pernicious thoughts. Then he gawped at her stupidly again. Any but the most basic vocabulary was beyond him.

"Well," he said, "we all went out with everything we had on hand, shovels, hoes, clubs . . . I don't know why . . . It must have been because one of us had one and we followed his lead. But then today, or sometime, I can't remember when it was, the priest said in church . . ."

But his speech had gone on too long. His mouth was dry and he had run out of breath, like a prisoner under intense interrogation.

"What did he say?" she asked with a smug smile on her lips. It was the first time she had smiled.

"He screamed that you weren't real, but a shadow of sin, then something about our sins . . . that then became real. Then he said a lot more, some of it was so awful that a woman collapsed right there in the church."

She narrowed her eyes and took a deep breath. She was giving herself time to think over what the man had told her. It was only then that the man was able to look her over, his first opportunity to inspect his find against a plain backdrop, like a collector of rare insects. But it didn't tell him much. It was like staring up at the sky when lightning is about to strike. He recognized it from the night before, when she had been a mere wispy ghost from his wife's past and he had demanded to see the adolescent girl with the small breasts and wayward heart.

"So, where are you from? What should I call you?" he asked eventually, trying to shake her out of her daze.

The woman seemed surprised by his question, as if suffering from amnesia. Then, after thinking back in vain, she eventually said, "Me? I don't know. Look at me, look at where I am. Phryne, I think that's it, use that from now on, just like I named Grisalba. Yes, I've named her Grisalba. You see? She looked up at me when I said it."

He was speechless, having never heard names like these, neither for women nor dogs. But he knew now that from then on, nothing would ever be the same; everything would be mysterious and different.

"And you?" she asked in turn.

"Juan," he said, a little shamefaced.

"Juan," she repeated, her voice lending full body to the word.

For a moment his name sounded special to him, invested with an importance and solidity that it never had before. But it was more than that: there was a remote echo of his mother in the woman's voice.

"Juan," she began, "I once . . ."

She stopped. She seemed stuck in a world without memory. *There is, in fact, nothing about her past that could possibly interest me*, thought the man. She was so much in the present, a blossom of the moment—may lightning strike him down for not knowing how to put this—and maybe a little of the future, but there was no going back. Back into the night where everything you once had is lost. Also—he thought further, still unsure of how to put it—there was this other thing, the nakedness of the woman so completely, passively visible, like a window open to the countryside. But that was as far as his thoughts could go; they didn't seem to be getting him anywhere. When he had imagined her in those feverish nocturnal hours, he hadn't wasted a second. His eyes had been shut tight so he would never lose sight of her, not even when he was asleep. Now, however, he seemed to be missing all the important details. He was caught in the bewildering trance of having her without touching her, like a melancholy eunuch, an image he'd never have associated with himself. He regarded her whole body as though she were a hallucination, barely noticing the dark triangle at her center that contrasted so sharply with the rest of her.

"Phryne," he blurted. "Why are you naked? Why aren't you like other women?"

"Oh yes," she answered, looking down at herself in surprise. "It's because of the story of my life, which I haven't told you because every time I try to remember it one or another of the details escapes me. I think it began like this: On my thirtieth birthday, I started to see the others as they would be in thirty years' time, their voices crusting over, their skin drooping off them in spite of all their vain efforts to keep it taut, treating sex as an abstract concept and living in fear of dying in their beds every night. So I made an excuse, went to my room, and undressed to inspect myself and see what was still in working order. But that order was meaningless: it hurt me just the same. Life hurts, in and of itself. And yet, suffering gives us no more rights than those without a trouble in the world, or any of the others for that matter . . ."

"Who are they? The others?"

"I've been calling them that since you joined me. They are the others. I don't yet know if I think about them so much out of hatred or love, no one has been able to help me with that . . ."

"So, then what?"

"So I put my clothes on a chair, like I was gifting them my former skin. Then I put on a coat and left for the train station, where I caught the last train that evening. The moon helped me reach that lonely house. I took off my coat and lay down on the bed. I didn't know where the light switch was, but I could see from what light filtered through the blinds that there was a book on the nightstand. It had a small dagger for a bookmark. That was when it must have happened. Because in the end my head was cut off, you see, and I was bleeding into my hands. I put it back on as best I could and went out into the countryside. I didn't have time to get dressed. After that clothes were of little use to me, and now I must be too dirty . . ."

"Woman, little woman," said the man, recovering his composure. "You're sick; you're imagining crazy things. You're not making any sense. And I can't take you home even though it's just a few feet away. As much as I would like to."

"Why not?" she asked bluntly. "Yesterday, I learned that anything is possible . . ."

"My God," he went on, tormented by his marital commitments. "How awful it is not to be able to do what we want. Even if it's the one thing you want to do before you die. But I have to try. I'll take you in my arms like it's our wedding night, kick open the door, make my way past the prying eyes of the house. Let's give it a try. But why do you cover up your shoulder, what are you hiding?"

She took her hand away to reveal a gash, like a claw wound. The flesh had been opened into two lips and the dried blood was furry with earth and blades of grass.

"Don't worry, Juan, it was just the claws of a tree. It hurts less if I don't let the air get to it. But it's not important."

"Yes it is, Phryne," he shouted agitatedly. "I need to carry you, I can do it. I need to tend to this and everything else . . ." He grunted to himself through gritted teeth, "She's a woman, a wounded woman."

"Juan, how will you tend to it?"

"I have a yellow paste," he said naively. "I use it when the children hurt themselves."

He realized that he had fallen into a trap; his clumsy words had blown up in his face. But the warmth of his proximity to the other being was too compelling to pay any attention to minor inconveniences. He watched her eyelids flicker, her delicate nostrils flare, the artery in her neck throb.

"No, Juan, don't pick me up," she said. "Your house is your home, which means it is no longer yours. I know that you don't understand, but I can't explain it to you. It's too difficult; it would take too long. Such things do not tempt me."

"Long and difficult," he mumbled, looking back over a story that had been his for so long that, like an old shirt, he couldn't remember where it had come from.

"Yes, but not long enough to forget certain facts along the way. If there are children to whom one must apply yellow paste, those children will be crying out for their mother. Also," she added, her voice taking on a more mischievous tone, "it doesn't hurt. I lied about the fresh air making it worse."

She'd turned her body a few degrees, and the wound was just below the man's chin. The feel of her touch rippled across his skin as she brushed against him. His lips fell on the injured area, wholeheartedly reenacting an ancient, violent, savage ritual. The iron tang of the blood sent him over the edge. It was like stepping out of his own, familiar climate into a gust of wind that would sweep him away like a seed on a strange summer breeze. And though his mouth, which now tended to a wound shaped like a woman's sex, longed desperately to enter through her true lips—what a gentle feeling it was, what a sweet, compassionate act. When he raised his eyes again, he saw that the woman's were shut, her mouth half-open. But this only lasted for a moment. She looked at him again. Her dark hair brushed against him, glowing with an inner light.

"Juan," she said. He was surprised by how her voice sounded. She took him by the waist. "What purity emanates from you, what unexpected peace I feel with you. Tell me, would you really have taken me home, the real me, without trying to give me another name like Antonia?"

Now he put his arms around her. Though he felt confident enough to be so entwined, the right words still eluded him. This woman made him feel stupider than ever: a useless fool. He tried to get out of his predicament by saying something, something silly about how much she must suffer as a lonely, neglected woman.

"No, Juan, I don't suffer," she said with a hint

of a smile. "But I would have enjoyed being taken with you, being with you."

The situation had started to become embarrassing for the both of them. They felt like old friends who had spent an enormous amount of time together. The woman still squeezed the man's waist, pressing against the top of his pants, which were kept up by a thin leather belt. How soft and feminine he felt; his hips weren't nearly as virile as his shoulders, voice, or chest, but they gave off their own sweetness, a kind of fruit that was too easily obtainable, available to anyone who wanted it, with no shell or rind to protect it. But she didn't share this with him. It was too intimate and perhaps offensive to the man's self-image.

"So," she asked, tilting back her head, still strewn with small leaves. "What would you have done with me?"

He roughly shoved her away, his jaws and eyes squeezed shut.

"So brazen! Women here don't ask questions like that. You end up making no promises and then not doing anything either. But, if you want to know," he went on, "I'd spend my days bringing you many, many things. You would ask me for whatever you wanted and I would obey. I would never forget and never tire. I'd bring you things you didn't even ask me for, things I didn't even know I could give you, and whatever is left of me, even though I've already given some of it away, as if I'd become a virgin again. But only to someone like you, someone like you and no one else."

"That sounds so lovely, Juan. I would only ever ask you for one thing over and over again. Even when you brought me water, I'd ask only for you, all of you, your pure mouth."

More than a desire to kiss her, the man was possessed by a kind of fatalistic death wish. He stood at the edge of a sky-blue pit that had suddenly opened up before him. He had no idea where it might end. He tried to step back, his dull everyday life, as embodied by the rumbling of the milk churner, tugging at the back of his mind. But regardless of his attempts to restrain himself, an autonomous, indomitable force drove him onward. His sex began to slither in its dark, warm nest beneath his rough clothing. It was so familiar, yet also strange, like being a child again but with a wealth of experience in your breast.

"What we give without uprooting ourselves we can give again, and maybe then it will be for the first time," he said out loud, barely recognizing himself in words that had sprung up like a revelation. And he understood them too; this was a new era in which everything—the world, the soul, and time—seemed to have turned upside down. Moribund clouds flew across the sky, crashing into the love-charged atmosphere with an explosion that coursed through her wounded body. Wounds that could only be healed with new, deeper, electric lashes, like horses of fire rebelling in the desert.

But then the familiar geometric sky, which had watched impassively as its earthly forests burned, decided to reclaim the spark and return it to its gentle, defeated, inert state.

"I saw something . . . something I never believed I would ever see," he said, collapsing against the woman's chest. "Your hair spinning around us. That could only happen with you."

They lay still for a few more minutes, each lost in their own reverie.

Then the man seemed to come back to the world he had escaped. He lifted his head slowly and stared at the woman in amazement or stupidity; it was very much like the first look he had given her. Behind that gaze, she saw, were the pitchforks, the clubs, and the sermon—two full days of lust and hatred. But everything he had known before the woman came into his life, he now saw in a different light, a light that radiated from her entire being: her voice, her hair, the wound on her shoulder, and her current amorous exhaustion.

"No," he shouted urgently. "No, I'd never!"

"Yes, Juan, you have no choice," she said gently. "You must do what so upsets you: hand me over just as your dog did before. See things the way they are, not the way we want them to be. They will come, and you will give me to them. I accept my freedom," she added in a new tone of voice, one that was quite similar, she noted, to that of a certain clothed woman named Rebeca Linke. "No one should be forced to suffer for the liberation of another, Juan."

"But I love you, I found you, I have had you," he said ardently.

"And that will all continue to be true for us, Juan, but not for them, which is what matters now."

She smiled encouragingly. When he saw her even, unblemished teeth, he lost his train of thought and asked a manifestly trivial question.

"Was it you who took a bite out of the apple?"

"Hmm . . ." she answered evasively. "That's an old story. It happened thousands of years ago, when I didn't even have a belly button. Why do you care about the damn apple?"

He looked at her uncertainly. His suspicions regarding her sanity were resurfacing.

"But don't worry, Juan. They can't take this away from us, not what we have, what we have shared, what we might still experience if you could only get over your discomfort. I will return to my house in the field and love you from there."

"You bought the house in the field?" he asked sharply, as though pricked by an errant pin.

"Yes," said the woman casually. "And I still don't know why. I think mainly it was because of my obsession with railways, but also because it doesn't have a postal address, or even a name. And in the end I wanted to please the people who lived there before me. I saw that the key came with the stories their bodies had left behind."

"But no one should live in that house," he said, airing his provincial superstitions. "Everyone who has lived there has died under mysterious circumstances. Afterward it never seems to have anything to do with the house, but it still casts its own spell."

She laughed out loud for the first time.

"Dying under mysterious circumstances, Juan? What do you care? I gave you my life when I confessed it to you, and you gave me yours, agonizing over not being able to give it to me. Maybe from now on that exchange is the only thing we can be sure of. It applies to everything that came before the poor cottage, which has done no more than kindly agree to witness our deaths."

"But you've bought it?" he insisted.

"Yes, of course. And they sold it to me without charging for the stay in the cabin, or my marriage to the river. And now I'm with you."

The man kissed her breasts passionately, burying his head in the valley of birth where all enigmas become clear and deliciously accessible. And this wasn't the only mountain pass to offer up its symmetry. He slipped both his hands down lower, exploring the geometric partition of the world where the other side of life was to be found: the damp, solitary place where the summer appeared to have taken refuge.

"Yes, Juan, my love," she went on, her voice faltering. "There will be a crowd armed with the same tools as before, but you and I will love each other and stay like this forever, far above their ignorant heads and their incomplete sky, a sky that cannot fathom what we have because we no longer belong to them . . ."

"Enough!" he said in an imploring voice, holding her close. "You can't imagine the trouble there'll be in the village."

They stepped back and shared a despairing look. Then the woman began to rub the man's chest with the palm of her hand. She went up and down and side to side with a childish joy, full of the promise of everything that might follow.

"I'd like to play with you, Juan. Will you let me? Some people never play, do they? How sad it must be to die and realize all you've missed out on."

And then the inevitable happened. They had both been waiting for it, albeit subconsciously, uncertain of how it would come about. Juan's wife walked down the front path with one child against her chest and the other, the freckled boy, next to her. The boy found the starving puppies, so young they didn't yet know what their legs were for, and put one under each arm. Then he walked around to the stable by the haystack, his small form now of immense consequence. At first he was struck dumb by his momentous discovery, but soon he was screaming news of it as loudly as his tender throat would allow.

☾

The Naked Woman! She had been reassigned her primitive, brazen, obscene name. The news spread like the pails of fresh milk being spilled by villagers not looking where they were going in their haste. It opened windows that had been nailed shut ever since her arrival, and brought even the most twisted, reticent creatures out of the woodwork to defend the family honor. The little man who thought himself a deacon forced the priest to hand over the holy keys to the church and the bell tower: he was no longer the father of their church, not after what he had said in his sermon. Until they received new orders, they would be governed directly, mainly by means of the bells. The sky looked like hot glass and seemed fit to shatter amid the metallic chiming onslaught the man provided as a counterpoint to the beating he had earlier given his chest.

The enormity of the coming storm began to dawn on Juan and the Naked Woman, standing out in front of the house. At first it looked like an invasion of ants or grasshoppers. Then, as the forms grew more human, they could see what each was carrying in their hand or had propped on their shoulder. The people had armed themselves once more, but they didn't yet know why: if they were going to kill the woman or the first man to take possession of her. If the latter, he would, with his dying breath, demand the death of the next, and so on, until all human life had been extinguished.

"Stop!" the man cried in an anguished voice.

He ran back into the house, grabbed the yellow waterproof cloak that he used for rainy trips to the stable in the evenings, and threw it over the woman, making her look even more fragile. She allowed him to drape it around her meekly, as if she were a child. *It might as well be the shell of the world*, she thought, but she didn't want to upset him with protests beyond his comprehension. He had done something subconsciously: whenever he put on his cloak he always grabbed his lamp, and this time was no different. The woman watched as, having set it on the ground to help her into the cloak, he picked up the lamp instinctively to defy the approaching horde.

The crowd marched down a path flanked by apple trees laden with fruit, some of which gleamed amid the leaves the way they do in postcards, while others had already fallen heavily to the ground. The two-footed ants had forgotten everything, even that ripe apples don't last on the branches for long. Everything except the woman, and now, of course, the cloak. Juan's stupid gesture had been like a slap in the face. Now that she was covered, they felt disappointed somehow. How could the Naked Woman they had dreamed of for so long have become this forest ranger with long hair and an effeminate face? But naked or not, there she was, finally, as real as Juan and his lamp, or the dog standing next to them.

The crowd turned onto the main street that led to the village hall, growing as it went. The buildings on either side began to spit out eyes, legs, clubs, and dirty words, not to mention a sizable pack of mongrels that perfectly suited their masters. The sun, meanwhile, had grown unbearable. The smell of the dry wooden houses, sweating trees, and cracked earth was overpowering; this was especially true for the woman's feet, which lacked the same resilience. Her wounds were raw. Her rest behind the haystack had barely helped, and now she was being forced to walk again over burning dust and rough, hypocritical stones. In addition to the cloak, she also had to put up with a sudden change in pace. She had been swept into an angry, suffocating world where for some reason she was supposed to wear a yellow raincoat. She rebelled for a moment, planning to shrug it off and throw it at her stunned entourage so she could continue on in her true form, the way they had first known her, but then she remembered the tenderness of the man with the lamp; she had experienced it so recently it could hardly be forgotten. Of course, he was no longer the same man as the one from the haystack, with his lovely waist, pure kisses, and desire. All that was left of him was a poor delivery man trying to shield her from the wolves with a cloak. She would have liked to look upon him as she had before, but was afraid of how much he might have changed, that he would now be a poor, terrified approximation. Just minutes after she had experienced true meaning, these ridiculous animals had replaced her man with a cheap forgery. They thought she was an imposter too. They were capable of making an imposter of God himself in their desperation to have Him cast judgment. But there was always the sun. She felt it in her wounded feet. It wouldn't let up for a second, and it would end up burning their fields, drying the udders of their cows, depriving them of every last drop of water.

Finally, the villagers arrived. She could tell from the change in the murmuring around her. Everyone was saying something different, and the resulting sticky mixture suggested that some kind of climax was imminent. The crowd began to convulse; everyone wanted to be at the front, to take the lead in the capital proceedings. *So long as it wasn't their death being discussed*, she thought sympathetically. *For that they'd want to be last in line.*

But what, in fact, were they planning to do? She hadn't considered this on the way here. Her lovely, empty head had had no time for the risky, futile business of analytical thought. The heat, a panting mouth, the smell of dry wood, painful feet, the fleeting temptation to pull off the cloak: that was as much as she had been able to process. She had been so ready to defend herself that she wasn't able to ask any questions, not that she wanted to. The only thing that bothered her was that the bells had stopped ringing over to her left. The noise had ceased suddenly, with a strange final clang, as if the metal domes had hurried down the stairs to see what was going on outside. The crowd was disfigured by the silence. The noise had filled it close to bursting, and now it was experiencing what a woman who has just given birth feels the first time she puts her hand on her stomach. But the stupor gave way to voices and questions: Who was she? Who was going to hand her over, defend her, judge her? The twins? Juan? His wife and son? The dog, perhaps?

Clearly, she was collective property. According to the youngest legend in the world, she had stolen someone's bread, bitten into someone else's fruit, and drank another person's wine. And they were all afraid of how she had chewed up their brains, how they had instinctively set out to hunt her, how she had incited all those bodies to look for her. A new madness was now unleashed: the appropriation of all possessions belonging to Juan, the man who had found her. The man's wealth was so great that even though his feat had transformed him into a kind of demigod, they could not forgive him. Their hatred of the twins lessened, shifted focus over to him. Now heads were merging together to outthink that of a single fool, their individual ambitions forming a new whole that would act in one voice. Juan unwittingly found himself at the center of a trance that was expanding at bewildering speed.

The woman understood the danger of their situation. Had she, a naked, destitute woman, really caused all this madness? Or was she being used as an excuse for something already lurking inside of them? Whatever the cause, the hostility was certainly intensifying. They came at Juan with axes, pitchforks, and shovels. She instinctively put out an arm to protect him: a pointless, childish gesture. The men, egged on by the leonine fury of their scorned women, knocked both woman and lamp to the ground. She got back up painfully. The general consensus seemed to be that this was the best way to cut Juan down to size. They dimly sensed that by dispossessing Juan, in addition to taking away his illicit wealth, they could disgrace him, make an example of his joy. The woman, in her nakedness, had reminded them too vividly of what they kept under their own clothes. The creature had cast a spell over their beds and unveiled the terror in their souls, laying their nightmares, resentment, and petty miseries bare for all to see. For a long time, they had been happy in their wooden houses, but now, suddenly, someone had told them about iron and glass. And one of their own was now the enemy because he had allied himself with this stranger's revolutionary passion. *If he protects her, he loves her, and if he loves her on his own, he is against us*, they thought. *We would have handed her over naked beforehand or taken her together.*

"Kill her!"

The stark, menacing words exploded in Juan's eardrums. He embraced the woman, feeling that she belonged to him now more than ever: an oddly intimate moment in broad daylight in the middle of the street. It was then that the villagers' hatred, only temporarily diverted, rained down upon his body. He collapsed, two blows from a shovel to the back of his head and his spine propelling him forward. They had to make room for him to fall to the ground, a lost pine in the forest.

The enormity of this event was too much for them. Juan lay injured on the ground, and several tongues froze in their mouths. But more knew just how to rile the crowd back up again.

"And now her! The naked beast!"

They were spurred on by a voice that, insofar as it was recognizable, belonged to the withered man in charge of ringing the bells. Their hammers, pitchforks, and shovels were raised once more. But then an unexpected cry was heard.

"Fire! Fire!"

They spun around like a collective top. For reasons unknown, whether because of the heat of the sun or an errant candle knocked over in the commotion, the church, wooden like every other building in the village, had burst into flames.

"Fire! Fire!"

They knew that fire couldn't possibly be extinguished by more fire, but still they spat the word back at the flames. It had all happened too fast. Now that they'd taken a moment to work out what was going on, it was all they could do to scream their heads off.

The priest, a disgraced judge in a trial where he was also one of the accused, had been forced to observe events from the village hall. But it was his home that was burning. "Yes, fire, that is all you know!" he cried with righteous fury. They antagonized heaven and then bleated at the sky like sheep to slaughter. He was going to show them what the love of God, and John, and Peter truly was. But not covered in the cloth of lies. He would go naked too, as naked as she, the woman who was offering them the milk and honey of the Song of Songs.

"Hold him back, he's gone mad!"

It was the same voice again, but now with a more shrill, feminine tone.

"Yes, hold me back if you can!" he seethed, knocking down a burly pair of peasants who had tried to pin his arms. "Let he who dares try to stop me!"

On the street, he began removing his clothes in the red glow of the flames, casting his garments in all directions: a rose caught in a whirlwind. A bony, olive body emerged, his chest and belly hollowed out, as though their bodily functions had been passed on to the curve of his spine. The skinny, naked man looked so pathetic, and yet so holy, that in the few moments he could be seen before he plunged into the flames, he reminded the bystanders of a defenseless, tender creature on its way back to a less arid world. The flames shot out beyond the building, threatening to devour the bushes in front. The village consciousness began to become aware of the real danger. From twig to twig, tree to tree, roof to roof, the whole settlement might be consumed. While crazy trials were being held in the street, their homes would be on the pyre. One man ran into his house to rescue a newborn baby, and then everyone followed suit, dispersing in all directions to protect the timber for which they had given so much.

The two prisoners were left alone next to the burning church, the gray-and-white dog still licking her prone master's face.

☾

The woodsman's wife was lost in thought at the edge of the forest. In some ways, this forest without fences or warning signs was her prison. The last row of trees had often seemed to her like bars. But the truth was that there were certain things, nonsensical for the most part, that her brain would never be able to understand. In her small, orderly world, she had assigned a use, label, or fate to everything she could: the number of healthy trees, the ones that needed to be replaced, the buttons on her husband's tartan shirt, the wine and cheese that needed to be stored, the faulty chimney damper, et cetera. And she didn't have much in the way of ambition, nothing that couldn't be achieved in the short day and miserable night that followed. Lately, however, her husband, a creature who never got lost and never changed, had begun to fail her. Healthy and well-fed, with those repugnant old desires now thankfully calmed, he had embarked upon a strange phase of hallucinations, a shameful, indescribable condition—indescribable because the right word did not exist. It was looking like it could be the end of one or the both of them when, an unimaginative being though she was, her mind came to the rescue: *You only get one chance to decline next to your man, you only grow old together once, you can't draw on experience. So you have to speculate and use your imagination. Maybe they were at a critical juncture in their lives,* it occurred to her one sleepless night. *Why shouldn't men also suffer the effects of age? It does nothing but wear them down and sap at their vitality.* And so she took responsibility for what would be her final duty. She learned to revel in the silences and to disappear like a ghost if he insisted on involving her in his senile deliriums.

She also had the option of escaping to the edge

of the forest to look out impassively at the old village like she was observing an alternative reality. From there, she acquired a border guard's instincts, which she enjoyed honing when her husband was close by planting or cutting down trees.

"Nathaniel!" she called to him. "Something's going on in town. The bells were ringing until just a moment ago. And now there's smoke, black smoke."

He went on chopping. He chopped with fury, almost hatred, at the light triangle he had hewn into the trunk. As he drew the ax back from the wound in which the tree revealed its true age, his whole body was infused with a desperate tension; he was so brutally alive that at times it seemed as if the tree would tip over out of the sheer force of will contained in his contracted muscles. But there was also an opposing will, a determination not to give way, to resist the low blows and stay standing. The implacable struggle was brought to an end by a humiliating noise, a merciless cracking sound. And so the tree's rebellion was quashed. The man had known exactly when it would come. He quickly snatched away the ax, wrapped a rope around the poor giant, and pulled savagely before jumping out of the way. As his old body swelled with blood, his adversary began to fall like a wheezing mummy with nothing to cling to. The air trembled with anticipation, listening out for the sound it had heard on other occasions, but it didn't come. The executioner appeared to have forgotten his customary woodsman's cry, which he still usually shouted even though he was the only woodsman in the forest. He stared at the log the way someone looks at a body, with a loving urge to etch what once was and never shall be again into his memory.

"Eve," he said absentmindedly. "Yes, Eve, her hair smelled like that of a fine woman. And you couldn't invent the scent that lingered on, some-one left it . . ."

He tried to extract the smell from that of the fallen pine. But the tree had left a dirty cloud in the air: bugs, dry leaves, dust, bird shit. And the uproar continued beneath the earth, echoing through vegetable catacombs, rattling underground skeletons in a chaotic tangle of roots—mass love caught in a blind embrace. He knew the phenomenon better than anyone. A tree is never alone, as much as it may seem like it. Like men, they laze about, apparently on their own, but under the ground they wander who knows where in search of company. Then they emerge with their distinctive heads to fool those who only know how to count in single digits, like a child in their first years of school. He, for instance, had also thought he was alone. He thought that he had spent thirty years alone since his search for company had ended in what he had believed to be a genuine encounter. But his companion had evaporated right on the very steps where they had been joined during that fateful ceremony. And yet, perhaps at the very moment that his asinine coupling for life was occurring, the other woman was being born. The woman from two nights ago who had bewitched his nostrils with the scent of damp honeysuckle. As hard as he blew his nose, he couldn't get rid of the aroma. But no more digressions; he was getting confused. The ground was still trembling from the felling of the pine, the shock galloped away under his feet. His wife was there, calling him over to see something happening in that damned village. If he didn't want to torment himself to death with the memory of the perfume, he'd better take a look. Perhaps his nose would be distracted by the bells, or the smoke.

"Can you smell it, Nathaniel? A house must be on fire; they're all made of wood and with the sun beating down hard like this . . . Poor souls."

"Good riddance, I hope they all burn!" the man spat venomously. "So long as it doesn't spread to the forest, so long as it's not our forest, let it consume them all, worms living in rotten wood! They can never have enough trees, always wanting more. More and more wood, damn it!"

☾

The Naked Woman knelt down next to her lover, who was now lying on his back. *His soft chest, half-open mouth, and staring eyes have a twisted beauty of their own*, she thought as she caressed him, wondering whether the minutes they had left together belonged to life or death.

"Juan, look at me, listen to me. They've left us alone, completely alone . . ."

In the powerful glow of the fire, they had both taken on the hue of blossoming apple trees, but in a remote spring from another world.

"Juan," she pleaded in a despairingly tender voice, "I'm here, I love you, I exist."

The words didn't seem to get through to him; he appeared to have long since abandoned his post. But suddenly, from the depths of the abyss, something infinitely sad began its reply, something that didn't feel connected to the man lying before her.

"You . . . I can't remember your name . . . You, me, us . . ." The voice came from nowhere, suspended in the air, ephemeral as a feather or leaf.

"Tell me, tell me what you want to say. My ear is at your mouth, and they're nowhere to be seen. Now, now," the woman implored him.

"I just wanted . . . you to take it off . . ."

"What? What should I take off?"

"That . . . ridiculous . . . thing I put on you . . . in a panic . . ." She understood. She removed the heavy cloak and threw it as far away as she could.

"Go on, keep talking, my love."

"Now," the man whispered. "Go . . . go . . ."

"No, never!" she cried. "How could I leave you now?"

Then, sensing that the entity that spells doom for us all was lurking nearby, she whispered again in his ear the way lovers do in bed at night even though they're alone and the bedroom door is closed. Then she kissed him sweetly on the ear. She was trying to slip him words and love through the only entrance still available to her. She realized how little she knew him physically. On the inner lobe, she had just noticed a set of tiny freckles. They reminded her of grains of sand in an oyster.

"Juan," she said again, hearing her words echo in the cavity. "You must live, to love me, so that I can love you. You never had any idea, not before we met at the haystack and not now, how much you can love me. My name isn't what I told you, or perhaps it is, along with many others. You would bring back many women, night after night, under a simple, common name, just the way you wanted it, because you would truly love them. You can't imagine how they suffer, all of them, how they have urged me to tell you this."

"Where . . . are they?"

"They are inside of me, looking out through me like rain on the window, lapping at their solitude like dogs do a wounded foot. They're in here too, suffering because they don't know how to uncouple themselves from love. They're like moths to the light. More and more of them will come out of me, each of them different, each with her own skin, smell, and voice. And if the woman I give you proves difficult to please, I would help you woo her. Between us we would turn her into a meek peasant girl, tamely offering up her little olive nipples."

"No . . . not now . . ."

"Juan, let me in, let me do everything that can be done between two people until they are indivisible, until we become one, one and no more."

"No . . . there's no time . . . go now . . . I want to see . . . your legs . . . from behind . . . from the ground," said the fallen man, his strength failing.

"No, no!" she gasped.

But she watched in horror as his face continued to fade away, drifting behind a film of sweat like a bird behind a cloud.

"Yes . . . I want to die knowing that you got away . . . Clean, brave you . . . They're dirty, scorched, and cowardly . . . It took dying to make me understand . . . what you meant . . ." he said, now bathed in sweat.

The woman saw how close he was to death. His tongue had no more strength left; it was making its final effort. Then, as in the most ancient of rites, she stretched out next to him, put her arm under his damp head, and kissed him on the mouth. She felt him respond very faintly to her lips. There was the point of no return, the boundary was approaching. And yet, it was possible that blood

122

was still flowing, the blood of love—a crushed, living rose.

Then, as if in answer, the only one his body was capable of giving, a thread of blood trickled from the side of his mouth. It happened suddenly, flowing faster than seemed possible for such a small stream. The woman was stunned by what was happening to him; it was a solitary, definitive shock. She wanted to scream, to shatter the sky with her voice, but what good would that do?

To one side was the fire, which was growing more and more ravenous, the murderers to the other. She looked back at the blood. Blood leaving the body brooks no argument, not now or ever.

"No, no!" she moaned with all her passion, for him, or herself, or perhaps for no one at all.

There was no more she could do against this grand denial, which is also the most terrible of certainties.

"No, Juan, no," she said weakly, barely knowing why, her eyes fixed on his mouth and the convulsions that racked his body, running through him like electric eels.

She rested his head on the ground and tried to stand. She wanted to grant his wish, the sight of her legs leaving the village. His static eyes wouldn't be able to see her back, but he'd know from her heels that she was walking away, naked, strong, and independent, the same woman she'd been when she arrived at the nameless village.

She walked away very slowly and deliberately to give her love full satisfaction. Love was dying behind her; perhaps he was dead by her fifth step, she couldn't tell. *Love has no future,* she thought, *merely a brief present, as fleeting as it is intense.*

"Tell me, Juan, talk to me from the upside-down world where you've come to rest," she said, still walking forward. "What should I do now with something I cannot refuse or give away? What does one do with love born with a purpose? Where, in what being, in what thing, can I deposit something created for someone else, someone who disappears without taking it with them?"

Bathed in a reddish glow, she looked up to the sky, a pomegranate sliced in half. She looked behind her. What she saw might easily have turned her into a pillar of salt or granite. The church had become a flaming skeleton, supported by a single pillar on the brink of collapse.

"Juan," she shouted, walking back. "The church is about to fall on top of you, I'll drag you away from there, let me pull you away!"

"No!" a voice roared from the ground, it seemed to come from all those who are not given a choice over the manner of their death.

The dog, still licking the face of the dying man like a wave lapping at the shore, rocked back as though she had been slapped. She sat on her haunches, whining uselessly.

And so, just as he had told her: she had to walk

away. But where? And what grist was left for her mental mill? She felt as uninspired as a cabbage. Perhaps she should follow the sun west. West. And suddenly she remembered. Someone had said something about the pain of man, all men. Something that would be useful walking any path in any direction. "My pain is the north and south winds, like unfertilized eggs laid by strange birds on the gales. My pain is like the death of my lover, it would be no greater if my neck were cut to the quick . . ."

She felt the painful mark left by the wire in her dream. "My pain is the north and south winds," she repeated.

Yes, that was where the knot was. She had to untie it. A pain that is everywhere and yet has no place on this earth, like the pain of drifters who throw themselves off cargo trains at places unmarked on the map. But it was precisely where they had to die for reasons they would never understand.

She had always hated morals. She rejected conclusions and the myths they create in a world that erupts suddenly like a volcano, like a landslide, like a silent shadow wandering in search of a crumbling body. *But at least the man who has leaped to his death in his dirty rags, his fleas abandoning his body as it cools, has brought an end to the cycle, the cycle that those settled comfortably in the seats of their first-class carriages never imagined existed*, she thought to herself. She had reached a location where life appeared to have forgotten its rush. She realized that she was on the rarely used path that led from the village into the wilderness, ending at the river.

More trees, more primitive pebbles under feet, bloody footprints. More uninhabited silence, the kind emitted by denizens of cemeteries. She felt the thick, sticky semen of the only man in the village running down her thighs. She remembered him once more, lovely and erect next to the haystack by the stable, telling her about his experience in her hair cocoon. Fear. This damp substance, still alive and full of power, and the creature from whose bones it came were one and the same. The only difference was that she could offer shelter to this small offering, while the person who had given it was lying behind her in irredeemable solitude, struck down by the cause. Yes, the cause. But in whose name? She wouldn't be able to explain it to a court if she were caught and tried. And yet, she must make a symbol of its message, she thought, a message that they can understand when they wake the next day, uselessly scratching their bellies, their eyes sleepy, a bitter taste on their tongues. No, it wasn't a dream, they'd say. There's Juan on a stretcher, one of his arms dangling down like an oar. There's his gray-and-white dog licking his hand, his fingers leaving a trail in the dust. Then they look to the church for strength. It's gone. They remember the priest's leap into the flames.

But there was also a naked woman, wasn't there? Now they're fully awake and she completes the trinity, but they still don't understand its nature. They don't understand . . . Suddenly those three words get lodged in their heads. In their efforts to suppress them, they multiply. Not because of what they contain, but the stickiness of the threads that link them together. More trees, more empty silence, more confusion over timeless experiences. But most of all, three innocuous words pounding away incessantly in her brain. Now someone had returned from some unknown place to remind her: a young man she once saw in a similar plight. Throwing a handkerchief into the air and catching it a million times until he was sweating profusely from all the pores on his body. "He's never done an odd thing in his life," squealed his mother to the men who came to fit him for a straitjacket. "But then he started this business with the handker-chief." *Each of us has our own handkerchief of madness*, she thought. But why this approaching darkness? Is it an eclipse? She didn't remember having stopped anywhere, not long enough for night to overtake her on the path. Perhaps the twilight came from inside of her, spreading outward from her soul into the shadowy landscape. She grew increasingly unsure of what was and wasn't real—as though everything visible were taking refuge behind shards of dark glass dropping out of the sky.

"Nobody falls asleep while they're walking,"

she said, using up her final reserves of inner clarity. "No one ceases to exist while their legs are still moving . . ."

"They don't understand." Sudden death had fallen upon the trees ranged on either side. Now she wanted to scream. But scream at whom? Everything was frozen. And what throat would she use? Then she began to feel the presence of the other. At first he was far away, but soon his footsteps grew closer, more real. They were slow, purposeless, like they had long ago refused to acknowledge their commitments, and, eventually, the body making them. It was the plough horse, or its ghostly double, which nobody had dared tie back up again. She was about to climb on top of him—he was the only thing in the forsaken valley she could claim as hers—when she saw that, from his hooves to his blank stare, he bore the burden of complete indifference. Nothing could now get through to him. But at least he was alive. Now that he was ahead of her, she could run to catch him, even with the cotton legs that had apparently replaced her real ones. Touching a real body could bring her back to the world they shared. Those people have probably driven it mad, the way you can drive an animal mad when it has been judged to have been in contact with evil. But surely he'll recognize the person who kissed his festering wound, fighting over it with that fly like a pair of widows squabbling over a lover. But even when she approaches him on her stupid rubbery legs, he walks on. He gets away from her again and again. Finally, after a series of such encounters, they come across something that will finally allow her to catch up: the riverbank. He has no choice, he can either turn back or wait for her there. Meanwhile, she will look back in time, to where she left her love, where the pain of the man of the four winds lingers on: *"Juan, the burning church is going to collapse, let me pull you away . . ."* *"No!"* The animal doesn't stop or turn away from the shore, but continues on through the water, its hooves somehow still dry, like Moses reincarnate.

Then she finally broke out of her three-word prison. She understood. The beast looked at her from the other side with phosphorescent eyes; it didn't seem as though he was only just noticing her. His gaze was that of someone who knows that the time has come for something, something that can only happen at the right moment. The river closed over itself and he stood there, eyes gleaming in the darkness. He was the only one still with her at the end, staring unblinking like a beacon of green light. But he was on the other side. And so she stepped into the water, her cotton, leaden legs propelling her forward.

"You fucking witch, you've changed the sheets! Where are the sheets? Speak, I won't let go until you spit it out! What have you done with that strand of hair?"

More cotton and more lead. A whirlpool swirling around a tangle of roots midstream, she can't decide what to do. She's caught in the trap.

"Shut up, Nathaniel, strangle me as much as you like, but just shut up! One way or another, I don't want to hear anymore. You might just as well squeeze the life out of me . . ."

Everything that ends up here spins around in mad circles, until some powerful living creature underneath swallows it up. Better that way. The triangle they never identified closes in a way unknown to geometry: the spiraling vortex with spinning hair and a circling female body. Then it sinks. Not so fast. A while later, in the blue time of the drowned, a rigid hand emerges, waving goodbye.

"Well, I burned them! Yes, I burned the sheets in the forest, at the foot of a tree. They burned like everything else of hers, like everything that belongs to the devil. You won't go through with it, you'll let go of my neck. Because I am the only witness, I'm the last memory of her you have . . . I know that you'll loosen those damned fingers . . . You need my throat so it can say no, she never existed, so you can go on believing. People need the disbelief of others to keep their faith intact and safe from the moths . . ."

Rebeca Linke and her long, loose hair passed through the forest a second time. She floated face down, as women with heavy breasts do. Bright violet in her last, naked state, in her final search for fulfillment, caught in the water's iron grip.

AFTERWORD
Elena Chavez Goycochea

"Who would you like to talk to, the teacher or the writer?" That was the sharply worded question Armonía Somers often posed to journalists seeking an interview with her. If they wished to meet the teacher, she would ask to hold the conversation at the Library and Pedagogical Museum in Montevideo, where she worked for more than ten years; whereas the writer would request they meet in her home.[1] In this way, she managed to split her life in two: Armonía Liropeya Etchepare Locino, the teacher, was born in 1914 in Pando, a small city in Uruguay, to an anarchist father and a Catholic mother; the writer came into being in 1950, when *La mujer desnuda* (*The Naked Woman*) was published in a local literary magazine under her pen name Armonía Somers.[2] Since then, the author has become a legend among Latin American readers and a challenge for critics and translators, so much so that it took more than six decades for us to be able to hold in our hands the English edition of her groundbreaking first novel.

Becoming Armonía Somers: A Woman Writer on Her Own Terms

The transition from Etchepare to Somers was a gradual one, as she managed to compartmentalize both identities, keeping them professionally separate for about twenty years after the release of *La mujer desnuda*. Living as Armonía Etchepare, she was a passionate schoolteacher and renowned researcher who published numerous essays on youth and education. Her advocacy for equal access to open-minded education led her to a successful career in public service, first as assistant director of the Library and Pedagogical Museum of Uruguay and, later on, as chief director of the Center of Educational Documentation and Dissemination in Uruguay. However, after publishing several other works of fiction—such as the collection of short stories *El derrumbamiento* in 1953 and the novels *De miedo en miedo* in 1965 (written in Paris while researching for UNESCO) and *Un retrato para Dickens* in 1969—Somers abandoned what she called her "civic life." By 1971 she had quit her job as an educator and devoted her life to her literary career. The shift toward a new identity was not only a strategic decision—Uruguay was in the process of transforming into a civic-military dictatorship in the early 1970s—but also an artistic statement that has endured until the present day.[3]

It was common for nineteenth-century writers to write pseudonymously. Generally, authors readily adopted pen names to distinguish the person from the persona, the private from the public. Women writers employed pen names to the same end, yet also used them as part of what critic Elaine Showalter has called the "assimilation process."[4] Victorian women writers, for example, adopted male pseudonyms to assimilate into literate society where writing practices were associated with masculine values. Such was the case with George Eliot—given name Mary Anne Evans—or the Brontë sisters, whose first stories were published under male names.

Armonía Somers's name change differs from these examples in that she was driven by a distinct purpose: the desire to construct a new woman writer, one capable of writing outside of social conventions and apart from any contemporary literary trend. Moreover, her gradual transition from Etchepare to Somers was motivated by her eagerness for freedom: "I realized how much more leeway fiction offered me in comparison to nonfiction, for I could play with that reality in a game that freed me."[5] Taking advantage of that leeway, her writing would ensure that women's bodies and sexuality were no longer marginalized in social debates taking place in the public sphere.

Furthermore, Somers's identity performance allowed her to approach language in new ways: for example, as a mechanism capable of conveying meaning through silence. As her narrator observes in *The Naked Woman*, "She learned to revel in the silences and to disappear like a ghost" (114). Paradoxically, the literary gesture of silence and identity performance entailed a protest, upon which ethics and writing were clearly intertwined in a nontraditional way.

> As I have said, maybe this decision was not only because I liked Armonía Somers as a name . . . or because it actually was a shield against any judgmental comment that people might make about me as a person who was working as a schoolteacher, and writing such things afterward. It was not only that, but maybe it was a protest.[6]

Although Somers never considered herself a "social novelist," nor followed the aesthetic of literary realism, she was clearly a social thinker following her own path. Her ethics and aesthetics put the body—mainly women's bodies—at the center of artistic and social debate, making visible what was historically overlooked. As French feminist Hélène Cixous pointed out in *The Newly Born Woman*, women writing about their bodies reveal in them a form of communication that differs significantly from ordinary language, which has historically been organized by masculine desire. This is clear in *The Naked Woman* when Rebeca Linke removes her clothes at the beginning of the novel, her naked body becoming a "cause" that seeks to defy patriarchal rules in society. "The cause? Yes, the cause," confirms the narrator toward the end of the novel. Departing from the myth of Adam and Eve, the Naked Woman demystifies and subverts precepts governing the body, often resisting and reshaping forms of socialization around her.

In order to further spark "protest" through her fiction, Somers adopted literary styles and techniques that drew upon everything from surrealism and stream of consciousness narration to nineteenth-century European and Latin American Romanticism. She was also indebted to the literary tradition of the fantastic, in which the unreal, the real, and the possible coexist simultaneously: moments such as Linke decapitating herself or communing with the horse. For taking such a radical, defiant stance in terms of her stylistic and thematic choices, Somers was often called a "parricide" by critics, implying that by not following in her literary forefathers' footsteps, she had in fact "killed" them—most being regionalist, naturalist, and realist male authors concerned with depicting sociopolitical reality through facts and detailed descriptions. While most traditional novelists followed the popular European school of naturalism—which used a third-person omniscient narrator to view the novel's action from a distance—Somers's narration instead moves in and out of her characters' minds. At times she adopts the Naked Woman's oneiric fantastic perspective or the preacher's religious anguish, and at other times she uses the voice of the narrator to observe her characters with a wry sense of irony.

Somers invites us to experience reading as a game of possibilities, playing equally with the ambiguities of silence and sound, nudity and covering, and darkness and light, preventing us from becoming complacent in the rigid structure of accepted thought. Even Rebeca Linke's multiple deaths are not simply the end of her life, as it is commonly understood in modern history, but the beginning of a new cycle. Somers's writing suggests, then, that the linear trajectory of women's lives has been a social myth that ought be transformed.

Opening Up the Canon: Gender and Genre in the Early Fifties

The foremost Uruguayan literary critic, Ángel Rama, considered Somers's novels and short stories part of a "secret cult among Uruguayan writers" because she joined a small group of writers who did not follow the literary trends of their epoch.[7] Her controversial plots and baroque style led critics to call Somers a "strange writer," even among marginal authors from the "critical generation," or "the generation of '45," as Rama termed authors who appeared on the literary scene between 1939 and 1969, before the rise of the dictatorship.[8] The critical generation, explains Rama, had a common agenda: to rebuild the cultural values of the modern Uruguayan nation. At that time, novelists such as Mario Levrero, Juan Carlos Onetti, and Mario Benedetti took the lead.

In the fifties, however, women writers were not easily heard within this cultural and political debate until they started publishing works with a radical aesthetic in which gender and genre collided: that is to say, when they took to writing fiction in order to talk more candidly about womanhood without the ordinary restraints imposed by male intellectuals, often their own husbands.[9]

One such author, from middle-class origins, was Paulina Medeiros, who published *Las que llegaron después* in 1940. Echoing the title, Rama said in regard to those authors not included in the generation of '45:

> Those who arrived later are women, who gained civil and human agency in this new society which they will speak of with fierce criticism—sometimes too rigid, sometimes cynical, always nonconformist—reformulating with more boldness than men those problems related to affectivity, and in particular, those of sexuality.[10]

While Rama acknowledges women writers' contributions to the arts, he still considers them secondary, when in fact they started writing and publishing in the early forties and fifties, to be acknowledged only twenty years later.[11]

Disregarding this blatant sexism, Uruguayan women writers didn't conform to establishment literary approaches; they took their marginalization as an opportunity to write about a different sensibility, more committed to an aesthetic of freedom in which a mix of traditional and new genres created a unique style. Understandably then, when asked about her relationship to her critical generation peers, Somers was always reluctant to be confined by such a label:

> I feel no ties with the generation I ought to be part of. I believe that apart from the usual generations, the literary ones are not only chronological but also imply a certain homogeneity of form, motivation, semantics, and even in ideology, that separates them from previous or future generations. In my case (not because I feel superior of inferior, but rather different) I do not consider myself to be part of the generation that they usually call mine.[12]

Alongside Somers, Uruguayan women writers such as Clara Silva (*La sobreviviente* 1953), Cristina Peri Rossi (*Los museos abandonados* 1969), Teresa Porzecanski (*El acertijo y otros cuentos* 1967), and Mercedes Rein (*Zoologismos* 1967) also constructed this aesthetic of difference and formed a diverse group that slowly brought this generation of women authors into the public sphere. Some of them, such as Peri Rossi, were even forced into exile after being persecuted by Uruguay's dictatorship. Interestingly, however, when *The Naked Woman* was published in 1950, readers could not believe it had been written by a woman. Somers had a clear explanation for their skepticism:

> They say [Somers's writing] has a certain strength, a virility, a valor that a woman usually doesn't express due to ancestral prejudices which are of no consequence to me. I believe it's good for women to gather, for women writers to assemble at conferences if they are going to discuss literature and not other problems. Besides, that spreads the news about our literature, which we ought to do since men are more prominent.[13]

Despite those initial doubts, today *The Naked Woman* is understood to have been groundbreaking, as its publication would bring down literary and cultural boundaries for women writers in the years that followed.[14]

The Naked Woman:
A Different Captive Woman's Tale

When *The Naked Woman* was serialized in two issues of *Clima,* a literary magazine, and later formally published as a book in 1951 and 1966, it caused significant upheaval in the Uruguayan literary scene. In interviews, Somers confessed that she would attend book clubs, hidden behind her pen name, just to witness readers suggesting that the book had been written by a man, a heterosexual couple, or a group of writers. They couldn't fathom, Somers remembered, that it was a woman who "dared to skip stones in calm waters."[15] As time passed, "modest Montevideo grew up and accepted the novel. Now that *The Naked Woman* is a legal citizen [of the Uruguayan literary community] there will be no further editions," Somers observed.[16] She didn't anticipate the future success of her book nor the posthumous Spanish edition in 2009.

It comes as no surprise that *The Naked Woman* continues to find new fans among readers today. This is the kind of book we want to read at night, far from noisy distractions, engulfed in silence, so that we are able to hear the voice emerging from the story. Eventually, the dark night herself becomes an eloquent narrator, confessing her lack of words to express what she is feeling and seeing. It is also the darkness of night that protects the Naked Woman throughout her journey, whereas daylight strips her of her power.

Rebeca Linke's personal journey demands the suspension of any rational skepticism and the acceptance of the uncanny mise-en-scène in which Somers's characters are situated. This entails an ethical awareness, according to which women's bodies and sexuality will be treated from a particular point of view: "I don't overlook these topics [of love and eroticism]; rather, I face them head on. I attempt an aseptic approach, not a celebratory one," Somers explains.[17] Early on in the novel, the aseptic narrator describes a woman's brutal rape by her husband in which he dismisses his wife's body completely: "He was oblivious to everything else, even the inert, pale, suffering body he was assaulting" (18). The Naked Woman's experience is recounted differently: "The woman left the cabin behind without ever turning back, not even to check if it had been real. She wasn't about to wallow in her failure. She had been a guest there and had wanted, demanded even, something they didn't know how to give her" (21). The starkness of this affective and aesthetic approach to narrative, even in scenes of extreme violence, demands that readers question preconceived notions and expectations and reorient themselves with regard to the text. Moreover, Somers's writing requires that we read with and examine a sense of humor and irony, while questioning social taboos, moral values regarding sexuality, religious beliefs, and modern scientific discourse on civilization. For instance, the description of the Naked Woman's beauty, as seen through other characters' eyes and desires, reinforces her otherness while peppering the text with sarcasm:

> They made their grand discovery: a naked
> woman in the middle of the field! They sat stock-
> still, their necks stretched out as far as they could
> go. It wasn't a ghost or a tree, but a real woman
> with long, loose hair and arms down at her sides
> . . . a wonderful woman such as this springing up
> from the earth, or appearing in the bathroom, or
> in the window across the road, offering herself
> in apparent supplication . . . (28)

The sarcastic tone, with its overblown grandiosity,
makes us consider just how women's bodies are
socially constructed and viewed.

Satire and sarcasm pervade the text, providing
both humor and biting criticism. The target may
be conventionality in any form: historical, social,
cultural, and therefore aesthetic, too. In an interview conducted in 1978 by scholar Evelyn Picon
Garfield, Somers points out how this strategy was
essential when addressing commonly accepted
beliefs: "You see, in me there is such a kind of reli-
giosity I try to transform into irreverence, so much
so that in my latest novel *Solo los elefantes encuentran
mandrágora*, I call God an atheist."[18] It is with similar irreverence that *The Naked Woman* effectively
undertakes the deconstruction of traditional feminine archetypes, often themselves imbued with
religious symbolism.

While these archetypes are dismantled in the
novel, it is worth noting another key feminine

figure, specific to Río de la Plata colonial history. Since the early nineteenth century, when Argentina and Uruguay were still taking shape as independent nations, tales of captive women emerged in the cultural imagination through literature and, especially, art. Such is the case in the work of Uruguayan nineteenth-century artist Juan Manuel Blanes, whose painting *La cautiva* (1880) depicts white women taken captive by indigenous men in *las pampas*—literally grasslands, but frequently figured as empty land and as a sort of frontier between civilization and barbarism. The rescue of the captive woman came to signify the rescue of progress and civilization. As scholar Christopher Conway observes, a binary opposition between civilization and barbarism

> was omnipresent throughout nineteenth-century literature and journalism as a justification for celebrating the modernizing (and Europeanized) agenda of liberalism and for denigrating cultural actors and elements associated with rural life and the colonial past.[19]

But counternarratives also existed, opposing the widespread idea of las pampas as an empty space and of women as passive agents. A well-known example among Argentine literature is *La cautiva* (1837), a Romantic poem written by author Esteban Echeverría. In this poem, María, a captive woman, and Brian, a Christian soldier, fall in love in the midst of las pampas while fighting against Indians. Brian is wounded while María tries to defend herself. She manages to fight off the Indians with a small dagger and escape, and, in the Romantic tradition, Brian dies in María's arms on the shores of the river. Both the nineteenth-century poem and Somers's avant-garde novel are laden with Romantic symbolism, where, for instance, the light of day and the dark of night become clear symbols of good and evil. They even share a similar ending. But Somers goes further by fundamentally questioning who, in fact, the "uncivilized" are when persecuting the Naked Woman.

> Soon the barbarian army was fully assembled. It seemed very important that they head out on their expedition en masse. Although the bounty would ultimately be individual, or at least impossible to divvy up, a sense of victory could still be shared and the presence of so many men served as justification in itself: they were a united front. (34)

The barbarians, suggests the narrator, are actually those Christians from whom the Naked Woman tries to escape. Unlike Echeverría's heroine, Rebeca Linke journeys from a so-called civilized Christian life to a new alleged freedom in nature. When she encounters civilization again after leaving her cabin—represented by the villagers, the church, the priest, and the town itself—she is fiercely persecuted.

This tale of reverse captivity is a nod to Latin America's colonial history, and shows how categories such as civilization and barbarism are contingent on who is telling the story. However, Somers was not the only writer who addressed a counter-narrative. In 1949 Jorge Luis Borges published *El Aleph*, which included a short story entitled "Historia del guerrero y la cautiva," in which an English woman voluntarily joins the indigenous people from las pampas. But Somers took it further, as she was the only one who subtly addressed this reversed captivity tale in her novel by telling the story from a woman's perspective.

In addition to speaking to cultural and historical shifts across Latin America, *The Naked Woman* can be read as an early symbol of Uruguay's transformation into an open-minded and egalitarian society through the acceptance of women's subversive writing in the mainstream literary arena. Even early critics of Somers's work, who maintained that she was not political because her stylistic choices did not conform to naturalism, later corrected themselves and acknowledged the subtle layers of social satire present in her writing. As a matter of fact, critic Ángel Rama became Somers's first editor, promoting her novels and short stories abroad.

Armonía Somers's life and writing were as inspiring in the fifties as they are now. She embodied everything a woman writer wants and simultaneously fears to be: innovative, rebellious, talented, and, moreover, free from the strictures of the masculine literary realm. Somers battled critics, reviewers, journalists, and the academic and scholarly demands of institutions, and finally succeeded at writing and publishing on her own terms. Renowned Uruguayan critic Rómulo Cosse claimed that the renaissance in Uruguayan literature was possible thanks to Armonía Somers.[20] Certainly, Somers shook the literary scene. Despite circumstances having changed since 1950, *The Naked Woman* is still a critical and creative call for resistance against the essentialization of women's experiences.

The first English translation of this novel serves to remind us of Somers's importance today, sparking new questions as to how traditional myths, taboos surrounding sexuality and desire, and colonial histories continue to impact our sociopolitical and personal lives. But the questions posed in this novel defy simple solutions. Instead they are open-ended inquiries, as it was Somers's hope that future readers would continue seeking new clues in her writing. This edition will offer the chance for new audiences to do just that.

☾

This afterword would not have been possible without Latina writer and scholar Mariana Romo-Carmona's critical input, Latin Americanist scholar Fernando Degiovanni's bibliographical advice, translator Kit Maude's comments on Somers's writing, Lauren Rosemary Hook's editing and guidance from the beginning, and Argentinian scholar María Cristina Dalmagro's thorough publications on Armonía Somers's archive.

Notes

1. Reyes Moreira 1959.
2. Somers 1950. The magazine is *Clima: Cuadernos de arte*.
3. I draw on the two publications that give accounts of Somers's trajectory as a writer: Cosse 1990 and Dalmagro 2009.
4. Showalter 1985.
5. Picon Garfield 1987, 37.
6. Risso 1990, 254 (translation my own). "Yo he dicho que a lo mejor no era solamente que a mi [*sic*] me gustara el nombre de Armonía Somers por que [*sic*] lo prefiriera, pues me dejaba un poco a cubierto del juicio que pudieran tener sobre mí como una persona que ejercía una carrera normativa, y escribiendo tales cosas después. No solamente por eso, si no [*sic*] que a lo mejor era una protesta . . ."
7. Dalmagro 2009, 95.
8. Rama 1972.
9. María Rosa Olivera-Williams (2012) explains how the fifties was a crucial moment for women writers, as they started to negotiate what a "feminine" subjectivity and "feminine writer" was going to be, as most of them were married to male writers.
10. Rama, 97 (translation my own). "Las que llegaron después son las mujeres, quienes alcanzan autonomía

civil y humana en esta nueva sociedad de la que se han de expresar con violentas críticas, a veces esquemáticas, a veces cínicas, siempre inconformistas, replanteando con más audacia que los hombres los problemas de la afectividad y en particular los de las relaciones sexuales."

11. While these women writers started publishing with a disruptive aesthetic in the early twentieth century, they weren't recognized until the late sixties, when women's rights movements around the world inspired a critical perspective on women's writing. For instance, by the time Somers published her first novel, Simone de Beauvoir had just published *Le Deuxième Sexe* in 1949. It's worth noting how writers such as Mexican authors Elena Garro and Rosario Castellanos were writing on the margins in the sixties, too, while Argentinian Silvina Ocampo and her sister Victoria Ocampo published the influential literary magazine *Sur* in Buenos Aires in the 1930s. Mexico, Argentina, and Uruguay, however, were considered the most advanced Latin American countries in terms of women's rights, while women writers from other countries in the region were kept in the shadows until the late eighties and nineties. For a detailed genealogy of female authorship in the twentieth century, see Olivera-Williams 1991 and 2012.

12. Picon Garfield, 38.

13. Picon Garfield, 48.

14. According to Ángel Rama (1972), certain upper-class women writers from the Southern Cone, such as Silvina Ocampo from Argentina and Clarice Lispector from Brazil, were often included in "official" literary circuits, and their writings had been canonically considered avant-garde. Somers's work, however, remained marginalized for a long time.

15. Risso, 254.

16. Gandolfo 1986 (translation my own). "Entretanto la
    púdica Montevideo creció y lo aceptó. Y ahora que *La
    mujer desnuda* es ciudadana legal no hay reediciones."
17. Gandolfo (translation my own). "Es decir que no miro al
    sesgo el tema, sino de frente. Lo que procuro es el trata-
    miento aséptico, no el regodeo."
18. Picon Garfield, 42.
19. Conway 2015, 117.
20. Cosse 1988.

Works Cited

Cixous, Hélène, and Catherine Clément. 2008. *The Newly Born Woman.* Translated by Betsy Wing. Minneapolis: University of Minnesota Press.

Conway, Christopher. 2015. "Gender Iconoclasm and Aesthetics in Esteban Echeverría's *La cautiva* and the Captivity Paintings of Juan Manuel Blanes." *Decimonónica: Journal of Nineteenth Century Hispanic Cultural Production* 12 (1): 117–33.

Cosse, Rómulo. 1988. "Del horror y la belleza." In *La rebelión de la flor: Antología personal* by Armonía Somers, 3–7. Montevideo, Uruguay: Librería Linardi y Risso.

———, ed. 1990: *Armonía Somers: Papeles Críticos; Cuarenta años de literatura.* Montevideo, Uruguay: Librería Linardi y Risso.

Dalmagro, María Cristina. 2009. *Desde los umbrales de la memoria: Ficción autobiográfica en Armonía Somers.* Montevideo, Uruguay: Biblioteca Nacional de Uruguay.

Gandolfo, Elvio. 1986. "Un país pequeño, una gran novelista: Para conocer a Armonía Somers." *Clarín,* January 9.

Olivera-Williams, María Rosa. 1991. "La mujer desnuda como manifestación de la narrativa imaginaria." In *Armonía Somers: Papeles Críticos: Cuarenta años de literatura,* edited by Rómulo Cosse, 159–72. Montevideo, Uruguay: Librería Linardi y Risso.

———. 2012. *El arte de crear lo femenino: Ficción, género e historia del Cono Sur.* Santiago, Chile: Cuarto Propio.

Picon Garfield, Evelyn. 1987. *Women's Voices from Latin America: Interviews with Six Contemporary Authors.* Detroit, MI: Wayne State University Press.

Rama, Ángel. 1972. *La generación crítica: 1939–1969.* Montevideo, Uruguay: Arca.

Reyes Moreira, Julio. 1959. "Dilema de una mujer singular: Armonía Etchepare de Henestrosa; Maestra y escritora." *Mundo Uruguayo,* January 1: 25.

Risso, Álvaro. 1990. "Un retrato para Armonía (cronología y bibliografía)." In *Armonía Somers: Papeles Críticos: Cuarenta años de literatura,* edited by Rómulo Cosse, 247–83. Montevideo, Uruguay: Librería Linardi y Risso.

Showalter, Elaine. 1985. *The New Feminist Criticism: Essays on Women, Literature, and Theory.* New York: Pantheon Books.

Somers, Armonía. 1950. "La mujer desnuda." *Clima: Cuadernos de arte* 1 (2–3).

———. 1953. *El derrumbamiento.* Montevideo, Uruguay: Ediciones Salamanca.

———. 1988. *La rebelión de la flor: Antología personal.* Montevideo, Uruguay: Librería Linardi y Risso.

———. 2009. *La mujer desnuda.* 4th ed. Buenos Aires, Argentina: Cuenco de Plata.

———. 2010. *Solo los elefantes encuentran mandrágora.* Buenos Aires, Argentina: Cuenco de Plata.

ARMONÍA SOMERS (1914–1994), the pen name of Armonía Liropeya Etchepare Locino, was a Uruguayan feminist, pedagogue, novelist, and short story writer. This is her first book to be translated into English.

KIT MAUDE is a Spanish-to-English translator based in Buenos Aires. His translations have been featured in *Granta*, the *Literary Review*, and the *Short Story Project*, among others.

More Translated Literature
from the Feminist Press

August by Romina Paula,
translated by Jennifer Croft

La Bastarda by Trifonia Melibea Obono,
translated by Lawrence Schimel

Beijing Comrades by Bei Tong,
translated by Scott E. Myers

Chasing the King of Hearts by Hanna Krall,
translated by Philip Boehm

The Iliac Crest by Cristina Rivera Garza,
translated by Sarah Booker

King Kong Theory by Virginie Despentes,
translated by Stéphanie Benson

Pretty Things by Virginie Despentes,
translated by Emma Ramadan

The Restless by Gerty Dambury,
translated by Judith G. Miller

**Testo Junkie: Sex, Drugs, and Biopolitics in the
Pharmacopornographic Era** by Paul B. Preciado,
translated by Bruce Benderson

Thérèse and Isabelle by Violette Leduc,
translated by Sophie Lewis

Translation as Transhumance by Mireille Gansel,
translated by Ros Schwartz

Women Without Men by Shahrnush Parsipur,
translated by Faridoun Farrokh